SO NEAR TO LOVE

Despite Emma's dislike of Mr Peirstone, schoolmaster in Ellerdale, she is forced to go to School House to look after his children. There she meets his son, Adam, and falls in love. But Adam's circumstances don't allow for marriage. Then Mr Peirstone dies unexpectedly and Emma goes to work for Dr Redman and his wife, Amy, in Ravendale. The doctor schemes to matchmake Emma and Adam . . . but can there ever be a happy ending for the young couple?

GILLIAN KAYE

SO NEAR
TO LOVE

Complete and Unabridged

LINFORD
Leicester

First published in Great Britain in 2007

First Linford Edition
published 2008

British Library CIP Data

Kaye, Gillian
    So near to love.—Large print ed.—
    Linford romance library
    1. Governesses—Fiction 2. Love stories
    2. Large type books
    I. Title
    823.9'14 [F]

    ISBN 978–1–84782–183–6

Published by
F. A. Thorpe (Publishing)
Anstey, Leicestershire

Set by Words & Graphics Ltd.
Anstey, Leicestershire
Printed and bound in Great Britain by
T. J. International Ltd., Padstow, Cornwall

This book is printed on acid-free paper

1

Emma did not like the expression in Mr Peirstone's eyes. He was walking towards her across the school playground and his blue eyes, usually so stern, were showing a warmth which seemed almost an admiration.

She stood still, wishing the children would appear in the school doorway and that she could be on her way home with Joan and Samuel before she had to speak to the schoolmaster. But his voice was calling her name and she knew that her wish had not been granted.

'Emma Strickland.' His voice was deep and pleasant, lacking the usual sharp edge of authority which was to be heard in the schoolroom. 'How very nice to see you again. You have usually disappeared with the little ones before I have a chance to speak to you.'

'Mr Peirstone.'

It was all that Emma could find to say. She had to look up a long way to meet his eyes, for Mr Peirstone was a tall man, in his own way, very striking. As schoolmaster of the church school in Skeneby on the edge of the north Yorkshire moors in 1875, he was a dominant figure in the village, disliked by his pupils because of his strictness, but respected by their parents.

At forty-six years of age, he was a widower, dressed always in well-fitting dark suits and starched white collar; his erect posture and his head of thick black hair with no hint of grey, made him look younger than his years. He was not a handsome man, but his air of superiority made him stand out amongst those around him in the village.

As Emma looked at him now, she was tongue-tied and embarrassed, wondering why he was seeking her out. Had Samuel been misbehaving, she wondered?

'Emma, you have grown into a lovely

young woman.' His words came smoothly and made Emma fell uneasy. 'You must think of being married very soon and not acting as unpaid nursemaid to your mother.'

'Mr Peirstone.' Emma at last jerked out the words. 'I have to help Mam, she has been very weak since the twins were born and I am needed at home.'

He had touched Emma on a very sensitive point though he did not know it. She felt very strongly that it was her duty to stay at home and help her mother, yet a hundred times a day, she longed to be free of the crowded cottage, the constant washing and cooking, and the cries and quarrels of her younger brothers and sisters.

But the schoolmaster was smiling and his expression was enigmatic; there was a forceful gleam of speculation in his eyes. He spoke thoughtfully as he turned to go back to the school. 'It has been very nice to have a word with you, Emma, you have given me pause for thought.'

He walked away and Emma watched the tall figure in consternation. Why had he spoken to her? What did his last words mean? She tried to forget the admiring expression in his eyes, for at that moment, the children came out of the school. Her little brother and sister reached her and they began the long walk home.

Home for the Strickland family was a miner's cottage up in Ellerdale on the moors of north Yorkshire. It was one of a terrace of twelve such cottages built by the owners of the Ironstone Mining Company in mid-century and called Victoria Cottages.

The dwellings were of local stone, solid but small and within a stone's throw of the iron mine where the men and boys found their work. The atmosphere around the cottages was dusty, smoky and noisy with the constant rattle of the railway truck which took the ore over to Middlesborough.

Down below in the village of Skeneby, the air was clear and the noise of the railway was only a distant echo.

Emma shared the cottage with her mother and father and seven brothers and sisters, she was eighteen years of age and the eldest of the Strickland children.

After Emma came three boys who all worked at the mine with their father; then there were Joan and Samuel, both of them at school and running ahead of Emma now. At home were the twins, weakly, crying babies less than a month old, with Mrs Strickland no longer strong and desperately trying to suckle the pair and look after the family at the same time.

As Emma walked up the track from the village, she had a sense of being torn in two. She loved her brothers and sisters, but in her heart was a rebellion against the life she was forced to lead. Since the birth of the twins, she had taken the struggle of caring for the family on to her young shoulders.

She was a girl of courage and spirit, but there were times when she felt like a servant, toiling all day until her young body was weary and spent. Two things kept her from running away.

The first was her daily walk to the village, to go to the shop, to take and then fetch Joan and Samuel from school. The second thing came in the spring and summer months when at the end of her busy day, she would take a book and walk across the moor to a group of stones known locally as the Slake Stones. There, she could be quiet, she could read, she could look at the view across the dales, she could dream her dreams.

Emma's was a simple beauty. She was not tall and she was small-boned, giving a fine, almost fragile air to her face, but the very fragility of her looks hid a strong will and a determination to do something worthwhile with her life. Her long dark hair was swept back into a single plait and the rather severe style gave prominence to her beautiful large grey eyes which were her finest feature.

On this day, which was like any other

weekday, Emma felt the sense of gloom descend on her as the row of cottages came into sight. Joan and Samuel had run on ahead and were already disappearing into the cottage, reluctantly, she followed them into the cramped and stuffy atmosphere.

'Did tha' see anyone?' It was her mother's usual greeting when Emma returned from school, imprisoned by her weakness and the care of her twin sons, Mrs Strickland longed for news of the village and Emma felt a sympathy for her.

'Mr Peirstone spoke to me.' Her reply was almost automatic. She had no real wish to say anything about the short conversation she had held with the schoolmaster.

'Has that Samuel been playing up again?' Mrs Strickland sounded surly and displeased. 'I'll get his da to tan him one if he has. The boy's growing into a right handful.'

'No, it's not Sam,' said Emma quickly, anxious to defend the little boy who was one of her favourites, perhaps because of his high spirits and efforts at independence. 'Mr Peirstone just said he was pleased to see me. I don't know why he should have singled me out, I'm down there every day.'

Her mother managed a smile. 'Always fond of you, he were. You was quicker than most to learn to read and write and didn't give no trouble. Perhaps he's looking for a servant girl, him being left with those two little ones since his wife died. Though they do say as Mrs Garbutt rules the roost in that household.'

Emma knew that Mrs Garbutt was a woman from the village who went into the schoolhouse each day to act as housekeeper and to do the cooking for the Peirstone family. She was known to be a good woman and loyal to the schoolmaster.

Emma was looking at her mother, somewhat amazed to be having such a long conversation, also at the speculation her idle comment had made.

'It's no good thinking you'd get a place there, my girl,' Mrs Strickland continued. 'I'm not letting you go, you'm too useful here.'

Emma bit back her words and spoke stiffly. 'I've no wish to work at the schoolhouse,' she said. 'I don't like Mr Peirstone. 'I do respect him, but he is so strict with those little children, it is hard to like him.'

'But Mr Peirstone likes you,' her mother replied. 'Taught you to speak proper, an' all, he did. Here's you saying 'I've no wish to' when any of us'd say 'I don't want to.' You want to be careful, Miss Emma, with your grand ways and don't go getting ideas above your station.'

Emma made no reply to this ungrateful comment and said nothing of the dreams she had for her life; such things had to be forgotten until she was on her own on the moor and had the time and space to be able to think.

She left her mother and busied herself in the kitchen preparing the main meal of the day which they had as a family when the men returned from the mine. With four of the men earning, they could afford to put meat in the pot and vegetables were home grown and plentiful.

After they had finished their meal that evening and she had settled the smaller children into the bed she shared with them, Emma slipped out of the cottage to walk across the moor to the Slake Stones.

A narrow path took her through the heather behind the mine until she reached the open moor. Ahead she could see the stones, great slabs of grey dominating the moorland scene. The stones were part of the moor and part of her world. Whichever way the rain or cold winds were blowing, shelter could be found amongst the stones, all the problems in her life could be forgotten when Emma sat in her favourite place.

For this was the place of Emma's dreaming. Sometimes her reverie would take her to some little village school and she would see herself as its schoolmistress. For in those quiet and solitary times at the Slake Stones, Emma would bring her books; a few precious volumes borrowed from the minister at the chapel.

If I studied hard, she would tell herself, I could become a governess in one of the big houses in Bransdale or Farndale. But then, on those precious evenings, her head would nod over her open book and her daydreams would be forgotten.

Over the next few weeks, she still enjoyed the walk down to the school every day, but Mr Peirstone did not speak to her again for which she was thankful. She could see his tall, commanding figure at the school door as he let each child out, often with a rebuke or a word of warning against bad behaviour.

Sometimes a smile would break through his stern features as he said goodbye to a child who was doing well. He did not look in Emma's direction and she soon forgot the brief conversation she had held with him.

June turned to July and with it, hot weather interspersed with heavy, thundery showers and humid conditions. The cottage was unbearable. One Sunday afternoon, Emma walked up to the moor seeking the cool breezes usually to be found there. But even the moor was airless that day and seeing black clouds fast approaching, she did not walk as far as the stones and turned back, hurrying home before she received a soaking.

As she came off the moor and passed the rail depot, the row of cottages came into view and she stopped in her tracks as she saw someone emerging from her own front door. She stared and stared.

There was no mistaking the tall figure of Mr Peirstone, dressed in his Sunday suit as he strode quickly down the hill as though he, too, was anxious to avoid any storms.

Emma's mind was in confusion, and with questions and thoughts juggling from space in her brain, she started to run. In two minutes, she was at the cottage and in the front door, standing out-of-breath in the living-room where she found her mother and father talking earnestly to one another. They seemed strangely excited and unusually animated.

'What's he doing here?' Emma managed to gasp. 'I saw Mr Peirstone, didn't I? Samuel's not in trouble, is he?'

It was her father who spoke first. 'Nay, it's not our Samuel.'

But her mother could not stop herself from interrupting. 'Mr Peirstone came after you, Emma,' she said and Emma could see that her mother's face was flushed and disturbed.

'I'll not work for him,' Emma cried out. 'I'm not going to be a servant to that man however much he pays me. I know it's hard here at Victoria Cottages, but I'd rather be with my own family than in the same house as the schoolmaster.'

There was a silence. Neither of her parents spoke and Emma looked from one to the other.

'What is it,' she said apprehensively.

Her mother gave a nervous smile. 'Mr Peirstone wants you to go and look after Alice and George, that's his two young ones as you know ever well. They've only had that Mrs Garbutt since their mother died. He seems to like you, Emma, I reckon he's taken a right fancy to you. Wouldn't you like it living in the school house instead of here in the cottage?

Emma looked at her mother. Then she looked at her father and she felt bewildered; she was sure that they must be hiding something from her.

'What are you saying?' she asked and stared at her mother who still seemed to be bearing a stupid smile.

'Mr Peirstone wants you to help him look after Alice and George, I told you. He thinks you are a lovely girl and would treat his children kindly. You could do it, couldn't you, Emma? It's been difficult for him since his wife died and . . . '

'Stop it, stop it.' Emma could not help the wild shriek. 'I don't want to listen any more. I told you I don't like Mr Peirstone, I'll run away rather than live in his house. You told him that I was needed at home . . . ?'

Her voice trailed into silence as she saw a look of guilt come into her mother's eyes and she cried out again. 'What did you say to him, Mam, what did you say?'

It was her father who replied. He was a man of few words, but something was urging him to confront her, to take her to task for her rebellious mood. 'Look here, my lass, you just listen to me. Mr Peirstone's a good man, looked up to by all the village, he is. Fine looking gentleman, too, I might say. What's more, he's wealthy. When his wife died, he inherited all the money that'd come from her father and grandfather; and that's as well as Skene Hall where that son of his lives.

'Mr Peirstone mebbe don't need to work at school, but he does it as a sense of duty. He's a top rate schoolmaster and you know it.'

'He might be a good schoolmaster, but there's no need for him to be so strict; he even canes the boys who haven't been naughty.' Emma was almost shouting at him, but he took no notice.

'That's no bad thing,' her father returned. 'Children who came from that school are well-behaved and can read and write. What's more, he's very proud of his work and he's every right to be.' He stopped and looked at his young daughter, but his expression did not soften.

He then continued to speak in a wheedling tone which Emma couldn't quite understand. 'Now you listen along o'me, young Emma. Mr Peirstone speaks very highly of you, says as how you are an intelligent girl and would suit him very well. Even said he would help you continue your education so that you could read with Alice and George, maybe even help with the school if you were needed. You ought to be thankful to get such a good offer, there's no' many miners' daughters as can say she's going to look after a schoolmaster's children.'

Emma felt tears of rage and frustration come into her eyes. In that moment, she had forgotten the dreams she had nurtured to escape from the cottages. 'I'm not thankful,' she said. 'I'm not going to do it whatever you tell me. In any case, how can you do without me? Since the twins were born, I've done everything. How's Mam going to manage without me? She can't, can she?'

She saw her father look at his wife and this time, a curious smile came into his face. He's gloating about something, Emma thought, they've done something behind my back without asking me.

'What have you done?' she blurted out.

Her father was still smiling at her and she hated the expression, it seemed so smug. Then his words came slowly. 'Mr Peirstone has been very kind and generous. He knows what a good girl you are to your mam and how much we would miss you. He made a suggestion to help us out, we couldn't turn it down. T'would have been madness.'

'What have you done? I'm asking you again, are you going to tell me?' Emma could hear her voice rising higher and higher.

'Mr Peirstone will give us one hundred guineas when you go to him and he will send up a girl from the village to help us every day and he will pay her wages.'

Emma saw the self-satisfaction in her father's face and she could not believe that she had heard right.

She took a step backwards towards the door and her voice came in a scream of hysteria. 'You've sold me,' she sobbed. 'You've sold me as if I was a slave girl. I'll never forgive you, not ever.'

2

Emma turned away from her parents, opened the door and ran out of the cottage. The storm clouds had gathered over the moor, but it was not yet raining. As if in a nightmare, she climbed quickly up to the Slake Stones as she tried not to think, tried to keep at bay the thoughts which were threatening her.

As the stones came into view, she felt the first heavy splash of rain and she started to run faster, reaching her shelter as the lightning hit the moor and a crack of thunder seemed to strike the earth; then the heavens opened.

Emma was not frightened by the storm and she knew where she could find shelter from the torrential rain. She climbed over the stones and crept under an overhanging rock which sheltered her from the driving wind and rain.

Her thin blouse had got wet, but she

had hardly noticed and she clung to the rock as though she might receive comfort from its solid surface; as though its very hardness was something real in an unreal world. She could not cry; everywhere was wet around her, but inside herself, she felt dried up, drained of feeling, devoid of emotion.

Of all the shock she had received in the past hour, it was the last one which had given her the hardest blow. She could still see the expression on her father's face as he described how Mr Peirstone had offered money for her.

Who should she loathe the most, she wondered? Mr Peirstone being prepared to buy the girl he said he wanted for his children; or her parents, her own mam and da, her mother and father pleased and satisfied because they thought they had found her a good position and were doing very nicely out of it themselves.

She banged her fists against the rock and felt herself glad of the pain. It was a real pain. Not the dull ache of despair and disbelief which engulfed her. She wished that she could think clearly, but all reason had fled in her dislike and fear of the man who had offered money for her.

She noticed that already the thunder was rolling away, but the whole of the moor seemed to be illuminated by brilliant flashes of lightning. She quietened down and gradually felt the fierce beat of her heart subside. Then in a quiet moment, she thought she heard the sound of her name being called.

'Emma, Emma, are you there?'

She frowned, and then gave a quiver of a smile for it sounded like James, the brother who was closest to her in age; he had always been very fond of her and she of him. She stood up in her cramped shelter, but could see no-one.

'Emma.' The call came clearer and louder this time, and she knew that indeed it was James.

'James, I'm here.'

Then he was at her side and she was making room for him to sit beside her under the rock. From underneath a drenched black overcoat, he pulled out something and gave it to her.

'I brought you your shawl, Emma, thought you'd come here and I thought you might want to talk. I'm sorry, our Emma, about what happened.'

She looked at the familiar face, suddenly older and more sensible in a very comforting way. 'Oh, James, you are very kind. I haven't been able to think, it's so awful. I've just been listening to the storm. Has it passed over now?'

'Yes, still a rumble or two, but the rain's not so heavy.' He looked at his sister, her face white, her eyes large. 'Don't expect you to listen to me, Emma, but I'll tell you what I think. It's a dog's life you have at home with our mam and those babies and all of us menfolk. I don't think Mr Peirstone's as bad as you make out. I know we didn't like him at school because he was so strict, but I expect we were little terrors and we didn't turn out so bad, did we?'

Emma looked at him, a frown in her

eyes. 'Are you saying that I ought to go to him, James? I didn't expect you to say that.'

He was shaking his head. 'No, I can't tell you what's best to do, you're older'n me. Got to make up your own mind. But I do think it's a good chance for you to get away from home and you could go knowing that Mam had all the help she needs.'

He was quiet for a moment. 'I was listening to Mr Peirstone when he was talking to them. He was very polite and he sounded as though he really wanted to give you a good chance. Him saying he would educate you alongside Alice and George. And then, he needn't have offered to help Mam and Da, but he did. I thought he was very generous, thoughtful too, offering to send a girl in to help them.'

He was looking at her closely, then he got up. 'I've had my say, Emma, and I'll be off. Leave you to think about it on your own. You'll be wanting to be quiet, I reckon.'

She gave him a bleak smile and tried to thank him. But he was gone, climbing over the stones and running off home through the rain.

Talking to James had helped Emma. She could see things through his eyes and it was clear that he wanted something better for her.

But Mr Peirstone, she thought? She was still assailed by doubts, but she tried to think about it sensibly. The schoolmaster had done his best for her parents, the fact that they had grasped so greedily at the money was not his fault. They could have refused to let her go.

She thought hard, trying to imagine the advantages of the situation. She would be living in a fine house and she wouldn't mind looking after the two Peirstone children, she felt sorry for them. Mr Peirstone was very highly thought of in Skeneby as he was not only the schoolmaster, but church warden, as well.

Perhaps it would be sensible if she at

least gave it a try, she told herself. Then she gave a loud gasp. Whatever was she thinking? Was she talking herself into accepting this offer, making herself believe that it was only a change for the better?

In a flash, Emma made up her mind. She would go and see Mr Peirstone that night after chapel; she would soon know whether or not he could be different from the autocratic school-master she had known for most of her life.

She pulled her shawl tightly around her and ran all the way down the track. The downpour had changed into a dense, misty drizzle and she was glad of the covering which James had so thoughtfully brought to her.

She flung open the door of the cottage and the family looked up. In the following silence, she heard her own voice, loud and rather strident. 'I am going to see Mr Peirstone after chapel tonight, I will tell you what I decide to do.'

She fumbled with the latch of the door which led to the stairs and fled up to her room, collapsing on to the bed she shared with the children. She cried and laughed at the same time, the pent-up emotions escaping from her until she lay exhausted.

Emma had only one dress and she always wore it to chapel on Sundays. During the week, she wore the same black skirt which she brightened up with cheap blouses bought at the market in Kirbymoorside. The dress was a very light grey, made of stiff silk, tight into the waist and high to the neck and it suited her pale face and grey eyes.

She did not wait for the rest of the family before she set off for chapel which was a solid stone building on the edge of the village. Inside the chapel, she heard hardly a word of the service. All through the long sermon — exhorting them all to repentance — she was rehearsing in her mind what she was going to say to Mr Peirstone.

She knew that the schoolmaster would be at home after evensong at the church which was earlier and shorter than evening prayer at the chapel. She ignored the surprised looks of her friends and acquaintances outside the chapel and set off down the village street.

Tiny cottages clustered on one side of the green near Skeneby Beck while, on the higher ground at the head of the village were the gracious and more substantial houses of the well-to-do of the community. Between the two groups of dwellings lay the small shops which served the dale, and nearby was the school. The house occupied by the schoolmaster was positioned in spacious grounds next door to the school, but not attached to it as in many rural villages.

As Emma approached, she acknowledged School House to be a handsome building, three storeys high, square and imposing. The Ironstone Company who had built both the school and the school house, had obviously expected the schoolmaster to have a large family and had provided well for him.

Emma's apprehension grew as she walked up the short drive, and for a second, she questioned both her wisdom and her sanity. Then she found herself lifting the heavy knocker and minutes later, the door was opened by a young maid who looked no more than twelve years of age.

Emma made her request to speak to Mr Peirstone and was left standing in a large entrance hall. It was a room in itself, with thick red carpet and walls lined with glass cabinets full of fine pieces of china and porcelain. There were two highly-polished occasional tables which Emma guessed must have come from a previous age of elegance.

In her surprise at the elaborate decoration of the entrance hall, she had not noticed that Mr Peirstone had come out of a room at the side of the hall and was walking towards her.

'Emma,' he was saying. 'This is a very

unexpected and pleasant surprise. Do come in.'

He held out his hand and she put hers into it. He clasped it in a hold so brief that she felt none of the dislike she thought she might have expected at his touch. He appeared tall and elegant, and he was smiling at her politely.

'Come into the drawing-room and we will have a talk. I can guess that your parents have told you of my mission. I see that they are not with you, for which I am thankful, we can talk more openly.'

Emma followed him out of the hall and found herself in a large, square drawing-room magnificently fitted with the finest pieces of furniture of nearly a century before. China and silverware were in abundance and the walls were lined with pleasing landscapes in oils.

He was looking at her and smiled. 'I can see that you are admiring my room, not what you would have expected in a school house, I imagine. I have my dear wife to thank for my most priceless pieces, they came from her parents' home. Her father was a country gentleman of some distinction and came from a wealthy Halifax cloth manufacturing company.

'Her grandfather bought Skene Hall as a country residence and Jessie, my wife, was born there. After her parents died, she inherited everything and brought all the fine furniture from the hall to the school house. I am very fortunate.'

He drew up a chair for her in front of the french window looking on to the gardens. Emma sat down, half-bemused as he went on speaking. 'But we did not come in here to talk about furniture. We have more important things to discuss, have we not?'

Emma flushed as he took a seat beside her where he could see her face; she said the first thing that came into her head. 'You can see right up the dale from here, Mr Peirstone.'

'Yes, we have a fine view if somewhat marred by the ironstone workings, but they are the source of prosperity in this little place, are they not? Without them, there would be no miners; no miners, no children; no children, no school! So there we are, you will think I am being foolish.'

A Mr Peirstone with harsh words on his lips she had been prepared for, but here in front of her was a different man. He was both formally polite, yet friendly and Emma tried to face up to the fact that the Mr Peirstone in the school and the Mr Peirstone in his home, could be two different people.

She tried to concentrate on what he was saying.

' . . . and you will know that my dear wife died nearly a year ago. We were blessed with four fine children. Ralph, our eldest son, is a lawyer in York and he married Isabella Haughton not so very long ago. They rarely come to Skeneby, partly because Bella had been engaged to Adam, my son who is next in age to Ralph.

'I wanted Adam to follow his brother

as a lawyer, but Jessie left Skene Hall to Adam, though unfortunately no money to go with it. Adam was set on farming Skene Hall though he knew it would be a struggle. I was not best pleased with him and I am afraid there is a coolness between us. He was devastated that Bella broke off the engagement and turned to Ralph who did very well from his mother's fortune.

'Bella's a pretty little thing, but she didn't like the idea of being married to a struggling farmer; she very soon married Ralph and they are doing very well for themselves in York.'

He stopped speaking and smiled at her. 'I am taking a long time to tell you about the family, but I want you to know about us. At home, there are my two little ones, Alice and George. I call them little though they are fast growing up. Alice is twelve and George is ten.

'They will be at Skeneby School for some time yet and although I have done my best to take their mother's place, I think it is time they had some feminine company.' He paused and looked at her attentive face and was pleased with what he could see there.

'I saw you meeting your brother and sister outside the school the other week,' he continued quietly. 'I thought immediately that you would be the ideal person.'

Emma listened carefully. He was speaking very reasonably, even kindly and all that he had said made a certain sense to her. She even felt an odd sense of pride that he should have picked her out. But none of these things was helping her to make up her mind.

Then suddenly, the schoolmaster turned in his chair to face her directly. 'Emma, I have told you of the position here; we are very comfortable and I can offer you a good home. You are used to hard work and rough work, but you would not have to do that here. I have faithful Mrs Garbutt as my cook-housekeeper, she comes in every day to do the cooking and the maids light the fires and do the cleaning.

'I told all this to your parents this afternoon. They were about to refuse this good chance, saying that they could not do without you. I realised that I must make up to them for your loss and fortunately I am in the position to be able to help them. Perhaps they told you of my suggestion?'

He is expecting a reply, Emma thought, I must speak. I must forget my bitterness at their willingness to part with me for such a generous offer. This man in front of her was showing nothing but consideration and kindness.

'It was very kind of you, Mr Peirstone.'

'I will tell you of my plan and see if it will help you to decide, Emma. You were one of my most intelligent pupils and you were also industrious. I happen to know from my good friend, the minister, that you have continued with your reading. What I would like to suggest is this.

'You come here to School House not

only as a companion to Alice and George and to help them with their reading, but that on occasions you assist Miss Paige with the smaller children in the school.

'You will remember Miss Paige? I am pleased to say that she is still with us. She does need help, there are so many little ones. You would like that, perhaps?'

Emma was taken aback. Dreams can't come true, she was telling herself, it was just as though someone had opened a magic door. It is what I have dreamed of all this time — to be able to teach in a school.

She looked at the man who was opening that door for her; she met his eyes, he smiled and she saw nothing but kindness.

She saw the look of someone who was actually thinking of her own feelings, asking her how she felt.

That moment of his concern for herself, together with an expression in the blue eyes which was suddenly turned to a gentleness of manner, won her over. She could do it. He was not as she had thought, and she could not bring herself to refuse the offer of helping in the school.

'Emma?' Her name was a question and he awaited for her reply.

All she could manage was a gruff, 'Thank you, Mr Peirstone. I would be glad to accept.'

He rose and helped her from her chair, shaking her by the hand at the same time. 'I am very pleased, Emma. Now let me show you the house and introduce you to Alice and George. I have told them about you and they are eager to meet you.'

Emma liked the two children and the arrangements were made for her to start at the end of the following week.

Walking slowly back up the hill to Victoria Cottages, Emma felt bemused and pleased at the same time. It seemed she had misjudged the schoolmaster and she could feel nothing but pleasure at the prospect of living and working at

School House, together with the bonus of helping out at the school.

The knowledge that Mr Peirstone had paid her parents so that she could work for him, she would have to put to the back of her mind, she told herself. I will try and think of it as a favour to me and a help to Mam and Da, she decided as she reached home.

3

A few evenings later, all Emma's possessions were packed into one bag which James carried down to School House. She said goodbye to him rather sadly, but he gave her an encouraging kiss, then turned and walked briskly back up the hill.

The tall, rather large lady who opened the door to Emma was Mrs Garbutt and she was smiling. She had a lined, but kindly face, her hair was quite grey and screwed back into a neat bun.

'You'll be Miss Strickland who's come to look after Alice and George,' she said, still smiling. 'I'm Mrs Garbutt. I do my best for the family and have done all these years, but I'm thankful those children will have young company. Right lonely it's been for them since the mistress died. I'd got hopes of Mr Peirstone marrying that nice Mrs

Driffield from Ellerby once the year's mourning was up, but it seems as master can't make up his mind in spite of him visiting her regular like . . . but I mustn't gossip.

'You come along in, Miss Emma — that's what I'm going to call you for I don't do with being too formal — and I'll show you your room. Then we'll go and find the children, reckon they're out in the back garden somewhere.'

Emma was amused, she thought that Mrs Garbutt would never stop talking, but she was glad of the warm welcome and followed the housekeeper up the stairs.

'Mr Peirstone said as I were to give you a room on the first floor not up in the attics, that's where Aileen and Nance sleep, they're the maids and good girls they are, too, but the master wanted you to be next to Alice and George in case they needed you in the night for anything.'

At the end of a long landing, a door was flung open and Emma gave a gasp.

She was standing in a large room, comfortably furnished with pretty flowered curtains and a rug on the lino.

'Is this for me?' she stammered. 'It's bigger than three of us share at home.'

Mrs Garbutt laughed. 'Everything had to be of the best for the mistress, poor lady, but there, these things happen and I know she'd be right pleased to know that master had got you to look after George and Alice. You unpack your things and then come downstairs again. I'll be in the kitchen with Aileen and Nance, you'll find us all right.'

Left on her own, Emma felt as though she was living in a dream. She stood at the bedroom window and looked at the view over the village and up the dale. At Victoria Cottages, she had been used to being high up, but here she found herself looking up to the moor; to her surprise, she could see the outline of the Slake Stones in the distance. I'll still be able to go up there, and said to herself, I can take that path that goes out of the churchyard.

She unpacked her bag, went downstairs and found the children having supper with Mrs Garbutt in the kitchen, they both jumped up, excited to see her.

Alice, tall and dark, like her father, was the spokeswoman. 'Can we call you Emma or do we have to say Miss Strickland as though you were a proper governess? We are ever so pleased you've come, it has been quiet with just the two of us. Father says that you are going to read with us in the evenings. Do you like reading?'

Emma nodded. 'Yes, I do, but I've never had any books of my own.'

'Never had any books?' It was George this time, and with a note of scorn in his voice. 'We've got a library, it's full of books, you could read all day if you wanted to.'

Emma laughed. 'I expect I will have other things to do besides reading,' she said cheerfully. She liked the friendliness of the children and explained to them how she was going to help in the school.

On her very first evening and after the children had gone to bed, Emma sat with her new employer in the drawing-room. She felt rather nervous. Looking around her at the grand room, she saw him smile.

'I don't expect you thought to find such luxury in a school house,' Mr Peirstone said to her. 'I believe I told you of my wife's part in it when you came to see me the first time.'

'It's a lovely room,' Emma said. 'I've never seen furniture like this before.'

'I hope you are going to appreciate it, Emma. I want Alice and George to be brought up with a good education and good taste. I have chosen you especially to share it with them. I waited many months before I made up my mind, but when I saw you standing outside the school that day and remembered your intelligence, I felt I had found the right person.'

Emma felt uncomfortable at these

words and did not reply, but she had no need to as Mr Peirstone went on speaking.

'Now I must tell you what your duties will be. In the mornings, I want you to go over to the school and help Miss Paige with the young children, then after lunch, I will prepare a course of study for you and I want you to do some reading. In the evenings, when Alice and George have come back from the school, I shall expect you to read with them though I daresay a walk in the garden would benefit the three of you.

'At weekends, you will be their companion. Your duties are light, but I will give you one free afternoon a week. Do you understand all that?'

Emma thought she must be looking bewildered. 'But, Mr Peirstone, it is not work at all. I hadn't been expecting to be studying like that.'

'But you have no objection?'

She shook her head. 'No, I have been trying to study at home, but it has been impossible so I am very grateful to have the chance.'

'Excellent,' he replied as though pleased with her. 'I am doing it all for a very good reason which you will learn one day.'

Emma was disturbed by this statement and tried to ignore its possible meaning. She said nothing and Mr Peirstone continued, 'For the moment, this is your time-table and I would be grateful if you would sit with me in the evenings after Alice and George have gone to bed.'

'Yes, Mr Peirstone, of course, if that is what you wish.' Emma said the words quietly and firmly, but in her heart there was a doubt, a small feeling of unease. The schoolmaster was not behaving in the way she would have expected and she found herself wondering at words which had been left unsaid.

She managed to put these doubts behind her and on her first day at School House, Emma helped Miss

Paige at the school in the morning. She remembered Miss Paige well and had always liked her.

A young woman when Emma had been at the school, she was now in her thirties; short, capable and with a head of deep auburn hair which Emma had always admired.

'Emma,' Miss Paige greeted her. 'I am delighted to have you to help me. There are so many little ones these days, but I know that you are accustomed to small children for I have seen you with Joan and Samuel. I hope you won't mind if I ask you to teach the youngest children their letters, while I concentrate on reading and arithmetic.

'Mr Peirstone takes the older children as you know. He is very strict with them, but he really is an excellent teacher.'

Emma listened carefully. 'I will be pleased to see to the younger ones, I feel it is a privilege.'

Miss Paige beamed and Emma felt that she was going to enjoy being at the school.

'I knew you would understand,' the teacher said enthusiastically. 'I think we will manage very well together. I am glad that you have come to School House and hope you settle in. Alice and George have been in the need of younger company.'

Emma counted herself very fortunate and all the time she was at School House, she did not find Miss Paige anything but helpful and friendly.

Her life soon slipped into a pleasant pattern and Emma found that she got on well with Gilbert Peirstone. He did not interfere with anything she did and his only demand was that she should sit with him for an hour in the evenings after dinner. On these occasions, he was polite and sociable, interested in the reading she was doing and in the time she spent with Alice and George after school.

Her afternoon off was on Wednesday and it was her custom to walk up the hill to visit her mother who was usually pleased to see her and to hear the news.

Emma found that she was a much happier woman than she had been and was pleased that it was so.

Even in the weeks since Emma had left Victoria Cottages, the twins had grown into stronger babies. Then there was Lucy Knott, the girl from the village whom Mr Peirstone had found to help the Strickland family, she was both capable and willing.

When Emma left the cottages, she always returned to School House by way of the Slake Stones for she had found the path which led directly from the stones into the churchyard in the centre of Skeneby.

One Wednesday as she walked up the hill, she was surprised to see James standing outside the door of their cottage and she ran forward in alarm thinking that something must be wrong.

But James was smiling and held out his hands to her. 'I was hoping you would come, Emma. Mam told me it was your day for visiting.'

Her eyes searched his face. 'What is it, James? Why aren't you at the mine and you are in your best suit, too. Has something happened?'

'Come along indoors and I'll tell you all about it,' he replied cheerfully.

Emma was surprised to see her mother looking pleased and she wondered what she was going to hear. She set down the basket of baking which Mrs Garbutt had sent and gave her mother a kiss. 'Hello, Mam, what's going on?'

'James'll tell you. We're leaving.'

Emma looked at James and found that he was grinning at her.

'I'm going to look for work in railways sheds at Darlington, Emma. They say as it's good pay. Not only that, there's rumours going round that the iron mine here has only a few years to go and I've got to think of the future. If I get on well, then I'll look for a house for Mam and Da. The boys can work, too.'

Emma stared at James and then

looked at her mother. 'What do you think about it, Mam?' she asked.

Mrs Strickland seemed keen. 'It's bad at mine, Emma, and I'll be glad for boys to go on railways.' She paused. 'It means you'll be left behind, but I don't worry about that. Wouldn't be surprised if Mr Peirstone don't want to wed you one day, Emma.'

Emma stared. Whatever was her mother saying? The strict and very proper Gilbert Peirstone marrying one of his servants, she thought? She had never heard such nonsense and wondered if it was gossip in the village.

She spoke quickly and defensively. 'You're talking nonsense, Mam. Mr Peirstone has got sons who are older than me. He's an old man.'

'You wait and see, Emma.'

Emma turned with impatience to James who was smiling at her. 'Take whatever opportunities you can get, our Emma,' he said.

She nodded. 'Yes, I will. I like my work and when Alice and George are older and George goes off to public school as his father wishes, then I hope to go to York and train to be a proper teacher.'

'That's the spirit, Emma,' James said. 'We'll all be going up in the world.'

Emma reached up and kissed him. 'I wish you luck, James, and hope that you soon find somewhere for Mam and Da . . . though I shall miss you all,' she added.

James gave her a hug and took her to the door. 'I'll come and pay you a visit when you're Mrs Peirstone,' he said with a final chuckle.

'James Strickland!' Emma laughed at him and ran from the cottages, crossed the railway line and joined the path up to the Slake Stones.

As she approached the stones, she saw to her astonishment that Mr Peirstone was standing there. She stopped in her tracks, not wanting to meet him out of the School House and wondering why he was there when he should have been in the school.

There was no sign of his horse which seemed strange. She had gone too far along the path to be able to pass the stones unseen before she took the downward track into the village. She decided with some nervousness, to hurry past and hope to get away by just saying good afternoon to him.

'Good afternoon, Mr Peirstone.'

Her voice, soft and clear carried through the air and she saw Mr Peirstone turn swiftly to face her.

Emma stood still in astonishment as she met keen grey eyes which did not belong to Mr Gilbert Peirstone, but to a much younger gentleman.

The man confronting her was very tall with Mr Peirstone's dark hair and handsome features, but there the resemblance ended. It was not only the grey eyes and the difference in age, it was the clothes. Muddy corduroy trousers replaced the elegant suits which Mr Peirstone always wore and a leather jerkin was worn over a tattered shirt.

'Who are you?' whispered Emma, fascinated at the encounter and with a strange feeling of recognition.

The reply from the stranger came in a hard, rather abrupt voice. 'And who are you, might I ask?'

'I am Emma Strickland . . . ' Emma started to say.

'You are Miss Strickland? You are the Miss Strickland who . . . ' his voice failed him.

'I am at School House and I help Mr Peirstone with Alice and George.'

'I don't believe you.'

'Why shouldn't you believe me? And who are you anyway?' Emma knew that sounded very rude.

'I am Adam Peirstone.'

Emma drew in a deep breath. So this was Adam Peirstone of Skene Hall. She had known of him all her life, but had never seen him before. This was Mr Peirstone's second son, no wonder she had mistaken them at first, she thought.

She met his eyes then and in that gaze no more than a few seconds, there passed between them a current of feeling which Emma could not explain.

The stranger felt it too, for he put out a hand towards her then let it drop back as though he had done the wrong thing. He was silent and it was left to Emma to say something.

'You are Adam from Skene Hall?'

He nodded slowly. 'Yes, I am. Will you come and sit with me on the stones? There is a lot I don't understand.'

Without realising that she had moved, Emma found herself sitting on one of the lower stones and facing the man who had said that he was Adam Peirstone.

'Why are you here in the first place?' he asked her. 'I would expect to find you at School House under my father's watchful eye.'

Emma ignored his last remark and answered his question. 'I come to the Slake Stones whenever I can, usually on my way home from visiting my mother in the mining cottages. It is my afternoon off.'

'You mean you really are the person my father has employed to be a companion to Alice and George?'

She nodded, but said nothing.

He was silent and seemed to be thinking deeply. 'I had imagined that Miss Strickland would be an elderly spinster. Whatever is my father thinking of taking someone as young and as beautiful as you into that household?'

He put out a hand and took her by the arm, but not roughly. The firmness of his touch through the thin cotton blouse was disturbing her; his closeness was disturbing her, too, and confused by the effect he was having upon her, she drew back.

'Why would it concern you, sir?' she asked faintly.

'I'm not sure, but my father seems to be acting out of character. I had not expected him to employ a young and beautiful girl to look after Alice and George. It is not like him and I doubt his motives. I had believed him to be looking for a wife and had heard that his name was linked with Mrs Driffield whom I believe to be a widow. Are you by any chance, Miss Strickland, looking for a rich husband? Does it not matter that he is more than twice your age?'

Emma's eyes blazed and she jumped up. 'How dare you, sir. I will bid you good day.'

But he was still holding her by the arm and she did not want an undignified struggle. His grip tightened before he let his hand drop, then he started to walk away from her. But before he had gone far, he turned back to her and spoke stiffly.

'You know that I am at Skene Hall. Father will have told you so, I am sure. Maybe I have misjudged you, it seems to me that I cannot trust anyone at the moment, but I want you to promise me that if you are in any kind of trouble, you will come to me at the hall.'

'I see no reason to seek your help when you have been so insulting,' she replied and tried not to sound angry.

'Just remember,' was all he said and

then he was gone. She watched his tall untidy figure ignoring any path as he ran straight across the heather in the direction of Skene Hall.

Emma sat down on one of the stones and was silent for a long time. What an extraordinary meeting, she kept saying to herself, yet how could it possibly have any meaning? Adam Peirstone had obviously quarrelled with his father, he was never seen at School House. He was a strange, rough character, yet there was something fiercely honest and kind about him. She wondered if she would ever meet him again.

She made her way back to School House with the strange feeling that, in spite of their hard words, she would like to know Adam Peirstone better.

But the meeting at the Slake Stones and the events of that afternoon were to fade away from Emma's memory almost as though they had never taken place. For in the weeks that followed, Gilbert Peirstone's attitude towards her changed dramatically and she felt a total inability to deal with his attentions to her.

It was now high summer and the garden at the back of School House was a blaze of colour. Honeysuckle and wild roses flowered sweetly in the hedges and Emma loved the colours of the lupins and the grandeur of the holly-hocks.

The grass was roughly cut by old Ben from the village who came in to tend to the gardens, front and back. At the far end of the garden and under the trees, there was a sturdy wooden seat. This was where the garden met the moor and became a favourite place for Emma.

In the early afternoon, her duties at the school finished, she would bring her books to the seat, but she was aware that not a lot of studying was being done.

It was on a hot day in mid-July that Mr Peirstone found her there. She looked up in astonishment when she saw him walking across the grass towards her for he should have been in the school.

'Mr Peirstone,' she exclaimed. 'Is anything wrong?'

'It's all right, Emma, nothing more than a touch of dyspepsia. I must have eaten something at lunchtime which didn't agree with me; my stomach does play me up from time to time as you know. The schoolroom is stifling and I couldn't wait to get out into the fresh air. Miss Paige is managing for me, so I thought I would take a quiet walk in the garden. I had no idea that I would find you here, it is a most pleasant surprise.'

'Would you like me to go and help Miss Paige?' Emma stood up.

'No, sit down, sit down, it is only another hour before the children leave. I would very much like to sit with you. Are you studying?'

Emma looked shamefaced. 'It is a book of geology. I thought I would understand it because of the mine, but it is very difficult. I don't seem to be able to concentrate in this heat.'

He gave a smile as he sat down beside her. 'I will excuse you and you can talk to me instead. Are you feeling at home with us, Emma? The time seems to have flown since you first came.'

She nodded. 'Yes, thank you very much. Everyone has been most kind, and Alice and George are no trouble at all. I have to confess that I am having a very easy time — except for the geology, that is.'

'We will forget about the geology,' he replied. 'You can spend the time with me instead.'

She looked at him startled, wondering whatever he was meaning.

'You do like me, Emma, don't you?'

Emma had no idea how to reply. He had behaved towards her in a way which was beyond reproach, but she was never able to forget his harshness to the children, for the years had not changed him. In the school, he was as strict as ever and it made her feel that she would never know the real Gilbert

Peirstone. Yet she had come to like him and to appreciate his kindness to her.

'You have been very good to me, Mr Peirstone,' was all she said.

For reply, he took her hand in his and she was startled though she did not like to withdraw her fingers from the firm clasp.

'I think you will come to like me as time goes on. I am prepared to wait.' And with these enigmatic words, he got up from the seat and turned to help her up beside him. 'It is very pleasant to be out here with you, Emma, and while the good weather lasts, I think we will make it a practice to take a walk in the garden in the evening instead of sitting in the drawing-room.'

To be with the schoolmaster in the seclusion of the garden was the last thing Emma wanted, but she found herself unable to reply and walked silently at his side towards the house.

And so, the evening walk to the end of the garden to sit on the seat in the shade of the trees became a regular occurrence. Their conversation never again took a personal turn and Emma was grateful for this. She had been wondering if his words to her when he had first found her on the seat had implied that he was thinking of asking her to be his wife.

But as much as she had come to like Gilbert Peirstone, she could never imagine him as a husband. Yet both James and Adam Peirstone had hinted at the possibility and she tried to forget their remarks on the subject.

She often thought of Adam and their short and disturbing meeting at the Slake Stones. She wondered if she would ever meet him again. They had clashed on that occasion, but his touch had affected her strangely and she knew in her heart that she would like to talk to him again. But he was never to be seen at School House and she tried to forget him.

4

The weeks of summer were fading before Emma became better acquainted with Adam. She continued to make her weekly visit to her mother and was more than pleased to find that all was well at Victoria Cottages. James was doing well in Darlington and the rest of the family expected to join him very shortly. She always made the longer journey back to School House by way of the Slake Stones. On two occasions, she found Adam there watching out for her.

The first time, he took her hand in his and greeted her boyishly, the hard lines seemed to disappear from his face. 'I know when you come here now,' he told her. 'If I can get away, I'd like to come and meet you. Do you mind? I have to apologise for being very rude to you on our first meeting.'

Their eyes met and Emma smiled. She thought she would have been shy with him, but suddenly in their glance was a sense of nice familiarity almost as though they had known one another for a long time. She found that she was able to answer him directly and frankly.

'I do not mind at all, Mr Peirstone, I would be glad to see you here.'

He laughed aloud. 'You can't call me Mr Peirstone, I expect that is how you address my father. Can you manage my first name?'

She nodded. 'Yes, Adam, I think so,' she replied without any hesitation.

'Come and sit out of the wind and I would like to hold your hands. I've been looking forward to doing that ever since our last meeting in spite of our disagreement.'

They sat together in the shelter of the large stones and Emma felt at ease with him and it somehow seemed natural that they should be there together. When he took her hands in his, she did not draw away. She could feel a caring softness in his touch even though his hands were brown and rough, the hands of a man who spends his life working out of doors.

He whispered the next words. 'Emma, I think I am about to fall in love with you and this is only the second time we have met. I've been thinking of you so much.'

Emma felt startled and stirred by his words and gave a short and merry laugh. 'You are talking nonsense, Adam.'

'No, it is true. You are like a light coming into a dark life. I'd sworn never to love again.'

Emma believed his words and knew he was referring to the Bella who had let him down and married Ralph.

She recognised that with Mr Peirstone, she was always on her guard with a keen apprehension of how he might behave next. But with Adam, she felt differently.

She hardly knew him yet she felt at ease and comfortable in his company. Now he was telling her that he was about to fall in love with her and also that he had sworn never to love again almost in the same breath.

She wondered if she could ask him about his broken romance. He was referring to it and she thought perhaps he might like to talk about it. She did know a little, for Mrs Garbutt had dropped various hints to her, but she did not know the whole story.

She was curious about this man who somehow had the power to disturb her. But thinking that she should perhaps change the subject of his broken romance, she asked him about Skene Hall. Mr Peirstone never spoke of it, nor did he ever mention Adam's name.

'Tell me about Skene Hall,' she said. 'You have made it your home? We never see you at School House.'

'No,' he replied solemnly. 'Perhaps Father has told you all about it. When Mother died — she came of a wealthy family, you know — she left the bulk of her fortune to Father, a more than generous legacy to Ralph which helped to establish him in York, and she left Skene Hall to me. You know that it was her family home?'

'Yes, your father told me. Do you like the Hall?'

'I love it and always have done, but the trouble was that Mother left me no money and the farm was very run down with only old William Calvert there to keep it going. Consequently, it's an uphill struggle, but I shall do it somehow.' He looked at her serious face. 'Do you understand, Emma? Is it worth all the hard work to put the place to rights? It's not a vain ambition, is it?'

She smiled. 'No, Adam, I admire you. I can understand how you feel.' She gave a chuckle. 'I've got ambitions, too.'

He looked at her in surprise, yet he had guessed all along that here was no ordinary girl.

'Yes, I felt as though I was a prisoner when I lived up at the mine. There were so many of us and I was doing my best to help.' She told him briefly of her life in the crowded cottage.

'Then I had the chance of looking after Alice and George and now — well, your father is very kind to let me have books to study in the afternoon. I also help Miss Paige with the younger children in the school and I love it.

'I want to become a teacher, not just to look after children, but to teach them as well. One day, when I am older, I hope to be able to train properly and get a certificate to teach like Miss Paige does.' She looked at him shyly. 'Do you think I am foolish?'

She found herself pulled closed to him, his face against her hair. 'I think that you are a wonderful girl, but I gave you a warning and I give it to you again.'

'What do you mean?'

'It's not like Father to give a servant of his a chance to study as you are doing, not unless he has an ulterior motive. Watch him, Emma, watch him.'

She lifted her head and looked at him, he was very serious. 'You never come to School House, Adam. Did you and your father disagree about something?'

'We didn't exactly quarrel, it was more a coolness between us, so I don't come to see him. He wanted Ralph, as eldest son, to have Skene Hall and the money from Mother. He thought I should study to become a lawyer as Ralph has done, not to struggle to become a farmer. I think he was ashamed of me.'

Emma was shocked. 'But that is unkind.'

'He can be unkind, Emma, that is why I am warning you, though you probably know it yourself from when you were at school. For some reason of his own, he is being very kind to you at the moment and one day, you will understand why. In the meantime, you stick to your books and don't forget your ambitions. We'll make a schoolteacher of you yet!'

They both laughed and the tension of the conversation was broken.

'I must go now, Adam,' said Emma.

'Thank you for talking to me. I feel honoured.'

They got up from the stones and stood close together.

'May I kiss you, Emma?'

She didn't hesitate. Without thinking, she raised her head and felt the delight of soft sure lips roaming her face. Then the lips found hers and she was lost. He pulled her closer and she did not struggle, her only feeling was one of wanting to be held very safely in his arms.

At last, he broke away from her. 'Emma, you are like magic. All I want to do is to be able to love you. Go now, Emma, and I will see you again soon. Goodbye.'

Emma ran down the hill to School House knowing that she was late, but the memory of those last minutes with Adam stayed with her for a long time. They met regularly after that and became firm friends as they came to know each other.

Adam delighted in telling her of his

plans for Skene Hall and Emma knew that he was including her in his plans although he had told her that he would not be able to afford to marry for many years. This excited her because she knew that she was near to loving him.

* * *

The days passed and during those last weeks of the summer term, Emma was to meet Ralph Peirstone for the first time. She found him to be as different from his father and from Adam as could possibly be imagined and Emma guessed that his looks came from Mrs Peirstone. He was as tall as they were, but there the resemblance ended, for Ralph was fair-haired and inclined to plumpness.

His expression was open and friendly and he greeted her cheerfully when Mr Peirstone introduced them.

'So you are the young lady who has come to School House to look after Alice and George. I was very pleased to hear that they had a young companion. Ah, here they are now.'

It was obvious that Alice and George adored their elder brother and it was a happy visit. A few days later, Ralph came again and this time he had Bella, his wife, with him.

Alice rushed out to meet them and then the door of the drawing-room was opened and a smiling Ralph appeared with a beautiful young woman on his arm.

'Emma, there you are,' said Ralph genially. 'I want to introduce you to my dear wife. Bella, this is Emma who has come to School House to look after Alice and George. She seems to be doing it very nicely.'

Emma found herself greeting Bella who was smiling at her. She was dressed in the latest fashion in deep crimson overdress with train and bustle. Emma thought that the face below the black velvet hat ornamented with rather large and ostentatious feathers, was very beautiful.

'I hope you like School House, Miss Strickland, it certainly must be an improvement after a miner's cottage. I am pleased that Alice and George have you as their companion — or should I say governess?' There was a sneer in Bella's voice and Emma could feel herself getting hot and angry. Surely this couldn't be the person whom Adam had intended to marry.

'I like it very much, Mrs Peirstone,' Emma managed to reply calmly. 'But, no, I am not the governess though I do read with Alice and George in the evenings.'

'Emma, where is Father?' Ralph interrupted the exchange of words. 'He will want to see Bella and then I thought we might visit Adam at Skene Hall.'

'Mr Peirstone is in the garden reading, this is the first week of the summer holidays, and he likes to read when there is no school.' Emma replied politely enough, but all she could think of was Adam and the proposed visit.

She was sure he would not wish to see Bella and that such a visit would not be a welcome one. She turned to Alice and George and hustled them out of the room, saying as they went. 'I will go and tell Mr Peirstone that you are here, Mr Ralph.'

Outside in the entrance hall, she turned hastily to the children. 'Go and tell Mrs Garbutt what has happened and then stay in the kitchen with her. I will go and find your father.'

She ran down the length of the garden to find Mr Peirstone gently sleeping over his book. She roused him, and told him about the visitors.

He stood up and he was frowning. 'Ralph is going to take Bella to Skene Hall? Good God, Adam doesn't deserve that.' Then he took her arm and held it tightly. 'Emma, you probably know of the trouble we had with Bella Haughton as she was then. Adam has always been inclined to blame me for it, but it was more Ralph's doing. But I won't have Ralph and Bella behaving like that to Adam even if I see little of him these days.

'Adam is my son and he owns Skene Hall even though I did disagree with my wife leaving it to him and with no money to run it . . . I know it is past history now, but I won't have Ralph taunting Adam by taking Bella there.'

He stopped speaking, but he was still holding on to her arm. 'Emma, run over to Skene Hall and tell Adam what is happening. Will you do that? I know that you have never met Adam, but you can't mistake him, he is very much like me in looks.'

'I'll go through the garden and over the moor, it will be quicker,' she told him, breaking away from his hold with a feeling of guilt that she had kept her meetings with Adam a secret. But she had no time for such thoughts; she left Mr Peirstone walking towards the house and started to run through the streets and up to the moor.

5

Emma had never been to Skene Hall though she had known of it all her life. She followed a narrow sheep run through the heather until she could see the old buildings in front of her.

Although is was called Skene Hall, it was no more than a large, rambling farmhouse; it was a low building with stone mullion windows and Emma thought that it had an ancient character and dignity of its own.

She was out of breath when she reached the first of the outbuildings which surrounded the farm — stone barns as old as the farm itself. She had started to make her way over rough tracks to the back door when she heard her name being called and she knew that it was Adam.

'Emma, Emma, wait. Whatever are you doing here?'

Adam's voice was rough-edged with surprise and Emma ran towards him.

'Adam . . . Bella . . . oh, Adam.'

'Hush, get your breath.'

Emma had collapsed against his chest and his arm came tightly round her.

'Don't try to speak any more,' he said. 'Come into the kitchen and I'll wash myself, by that time, you'll have got your breath back.

She did as she was told and went into the farmhouse by the back door and found herself in an enormous low-ceilinged kitchen with not a lot more in it than a scrubbed wooden table, a dresser and just one chair placed at the table. The walls were whitewashed and she noticed that it was all very clean.

'Sit down there,' ordered Adam pointing to a settle in the corner. 'I won't be a minute.'

He went to the stone sink, took a jug of water and poured it over his head, then quickly rubbed himself dry with a rough towel. In minutes, he was sitting beside her on the settle and pushing his damp, dark hair from his face.

'Now, what's all this about Bella?' he asked her.

Emma had got her breath back and now that she was at Skene Hall, she did not know quite what to say to Adam.

'Ralph has come to School House. He's driving a phaeton and his wife is with him. It is the first time I have met her.'

'Bella?'

She nodded. 'Yes it is Bella. She is very pretty and smartly dressed, too.'

'But, Emma, you didn't run all the way over here just to tell me that Ralph and Bella had arrived at School House.'

She shook her head. 'No, I didn't. Mr Peirstone sent me. You see, Ralph said that he was going to bring Bella to call on you at Skene Hall.'

In the sparse kitchen, Emma wasn't allowed to finish telling Adam that Bella was coming to see him.

He had jumped up. Emma thought that she knew him well by now, but she had never seen him angry before. His black brows almost met in a scowl, his voice was violent. 'I'll kill him. If he comes near Skene Hall, I'll kill him.'

Emma rushed to his side feeling frightened. 'Adam, don't talk like that. You mustn't say things like that.'

'Why not?'

'Bella's not worth it. If you ask me, Ralph did you a good turn taking her away from you. She's so fashionably dressed I can see at a glance that she'd never make a farmer's wife however much you loved her.' She tugged at his arm. 'You must listen to me. Don't do anything foolish . . . please.'

He glanced down at her, saw her sweet worried face and gradually his expression changed.

'You are right, Emma, you always will be. You seem to know the right things to do, the right things to say. But I don't want to meet Bella. Perhaps I am wrong, but it's still painful for me in spite of the fact that I've met you now. But I won't be here, I refuse to stay here and meet them both.'

'Adam.' Emma stared moving towards the window, they were at the back of the farmhouse, and outside beyond the barns, the ground rose steeply up to the moor. A few fields, then the line of the heather started, purple and glorious at that time of year. Above that, the moor stretched as far as the Slake Stones in the distance.

Adam came back behind her and placed his hands on her shoulders. The touch made her quiver, but she gave no sign.

'What are you thinking, Emma?' he asked her and his tone was now quiet.

'What can you see from the moor?'

'What can you see?' he sounded puzzled. 'Well, from those stones in front of you. there is a direct view on to Skene Hall and you can see the track which leads from the hall to the village.

'In fact, you can almost see School House except that it's lost in a huddle of houses and cottages.'

He stopped and gave a low laugh.

'You little minx, I know what you are thinking. We'll go up on the moor and watch Ralph and Bella arrive and they'll find no-one at home at Skene Hall.'

He took her by the hand, roughly and urgently. 'Come along then, there's no time to lose, they could be here at any moment.'

Emma followed him out of the back door and through the steeply sloping fields and once again her breath was taken away. Adam paused only to help her through the narrow snickets in the stone wall which were built to allow a man through, but to prevent the sheep from roaming.

Once they had left the fields behind them and were making their way through the heather, he slowed down and she had time to look over her shoulder.

She could still see Skene Hall below her and just as Adam had said beyond was the whole village of Skeneby set in the folds of the dale.

Adam stopped at a group of stones

not unlike the Slake Stones, but lacking the size and character of Emma's favourite haunt. He dropped to the ground and pulled her down beside him.

'There you are,' he said triumphantly. 'We've got a bird's eye view. Can you pick out the church?'

Emma looked hard and nodded. 'Yes, it's not difficult because of the tower, but I can't see School House.'

He pointed. 'It's in that group of houses there, by the big clump of trees. Now look closely and you'll see the track which leads to Skene Hall. Watch carefully now. I will, too.'

They were both silent for a long time, sitting side by side in the heather, their backs against one of the stones. The only sounds were of the wind whistling around them and the plaintive cries of the lapwings overhead.

Then Emma gave a shout. 'Adam, look . . . '

She needn't have spoken for Adam, too, had seen the movement on the track as the distant speck of the phaeton emerged from the village. It could be seen more clearly as it moved nearer the hall.

Then it came closer and they lost sight of it as it approached the front of the hall and was hidden by the building itself.

'Adam . . . '

'Shhh . . . ' he took her hand. 'Try to imagine just what is happening. Ralph and Bella are walking up to the front door — it is never locked, by the way. They knock, but no-one comes so they go in. Ha-ha, no-one there, they give up. Now watch carefully; they are walking back to the phaeton, it will soon appear again and be on its way back to School House.'

It was just as Adam had said and they watched as the small vehicle with its frustrated passengers disappeared into the village once again.

Adam and Emma looked at each other. Their eyes met and Emma's were alight with mischief. They burst out laughing.

Adam drew her close to him. 'We've outwitted them,' he said and there was still laughter in his voice. 'Thank you, Emma, for coming to tell me. I shouldn't feel like that about Bella, she is Ralph's wife now and they seem happy enough.'

He kissed her then, a long kiss with left Emma breathless and with an excited emotion.

Then they drew apart and looked at each other and they could read only one thing in each other's eyes.

'I love you, Emma,' Adam whispered. 'I love you and I want to make you my wife, but it will have to be one day in the future. I have nothing to offer a wife at this moment; but one day, when I have made a success of Skene Hall, will you marry me and come and make your home with me there?'

6

Emma heard Adam's words as she looked down at the old farmhouse. Her head was against his rough shirt, she could feel the heavy thud of his heart. She could hardly believe his words, but of one thing she was sure. She loved Adam Peirstone just as he loved her.

His fingers touched her cheek. 'You are silent, Emma, did you hear me? I am asking you to be my wife. Will you say yes?'

At last she spoke. She raised her head and met friendly and adoring eyes, her voice was quiet as she gave her reply. 'Yes, Adam, I do love you. But, Adam, I am the daughter of a miner, would your father approve of such a marriage?'

'My father has nothing to do with my choice of wife.'

She still protested. 'And what about Bella?'

'Bah, what I felt for Bella was nothing to what I feel for you. You must believe me, Emma. Bella was so beautiful that I thought it was love I felt for her, but it was a love which soon turned to ashes. When I first met you at the Slake Stones, I knew true love at that very instant. Now that I've come to know you, I am not mistaken.

'You felt the same, didn't you, Emma, you can't deny it.' His arm was tight around her shoulders. 'Will you wait for me, Emma? It may be a year or two before I am able to offer a home to a wife. Will you wait that long?'

Shyly, she smiled up at him, but her voice was firm and true. 'Yes, I am willing to wait, Adam. I would like to marry you.'

'And you won't mind living at Skene Hall? You'll be the lady of the manor!'

Emma laughed. 'I think I shall be a farmer's wife,' she said. 'But I would like that and the hall is a lovely place, I would like to live there.'

'What about this idea of yours of

becoming a teacher though?'

'Oh, Adam, I suppose it was just day-dreaming, and I hadn't met you then. You come first in my life from now on.' Emma spoke sincerely and felt very certain of her feelings.

'So in the meantime, you'll stay with Father at School House? You will be near me then and we can meet often.' As he spoke, he pulled her close against him. 'One more kiss to tell me that you are mine and then I want us to go back to Skene Hall. I have something to give you.'

They kissed solemnly and briefly, it was a pledge to each other. They walked slowly back to the hall, Adam's arm around Emma's waist. She had the rather pleasing feeling that it was proper that it should be so.

★ ★ ★

In the kitchen, he made her sit on the settle again. 'Stay there for a minute while I fetch something,' he told her.

He went out of the kitchen and she heard him open a door at the front of the house. He was soon back and held something in his hand.

He opened his fingers and she saw, lying in the palm of his hand, a pendant on a chain. It was a small opal set in gold.

'I want you to have this.' He was speaking very quietly. 'It belonged to my grandmother, I was very fond of her. I never showed it to Bella, it wasn't her style and I had to buy her a flashy ring. I suppose that should have warned me now I come to think about it. But forget Bella, this is for you.'

She looked at the pendant and then up at him. 'I shouldn't be taking something that is precious to you, Adam. Did your grandmother live here at Skene Hall?'

'Yes, it was a lovely house in her day and before she died, she gave me this. I have always treasured it and I want you to have it. Will you let me put it round your neck?'

She stood before him and he slipped the chain over her head, then placed the pendant in the opening of her dress she felt it cold against her skin.

'I feel honoured, Adam, and I will always wear it to remind me of you when I can't see you, but I won't let it be seen.'

He kissed her forehead. 'Thank you, Emma, you had better be on your way now or Father will be wondering what has become of you. I think Ralph will have taken Bella back to York by now.

'Listen, Emma, I will go to the Slake Stones whenever I can on your afternoon off; if I am not there, you will know that it is because it is harvest time and I can't get away. But I will be thinking of you.'

They said goodbye and Emma hurried back to School House taking the shorter route through the village.

Her head was in the clouds, her fingers kept straying to the pendant under her dress and she thought she had never been so happy.

That same evening, with joy in her heart at the thought of Adam, Emma found herself facing a Peirstone who seemed to be in a strange mood. When dinner was over — he dined on his own — he sent for Emma. She joined him in the drawing-room.

'There you are, my dear,' he said, smiling at her. 'Go and have your supper with the children, then join me in the garden. There is something I want to say to you and I think you might put on one of your nice dresses.'

Emma went away puzzled by the last remark. When she had come to School House from Victoria Cottages, Gilbert Peirstone had insisted that she went with Mrs Garbutt into Kirbymoorside with the weekly carrier.

He gave her enough money to buy herself clothes. She had felt embarrassed at accepting the money at the time, but realised that he did not want her to be seen in his children's company wearing only the poor blouses and black stuff skirt that she had brought with her.

Mrs Garbutt had helped her to choose sensibly and when they returned to Skeneby, Mr Peirstone had insisted on seeing their purchases and he had seemed pleased with the dresses they had chosen.

So later that evening and without knowing why the schoolmaster had requested it, Emma put on her favourite dress of a soft lilac cotton patterned with tiny springs of flowers. She knew that it suited her.

When she reached the seat at the bottom of the garden on a still and warm evening, Emma thought that Mr Peirstone looked pale and rather tired. She expressed concern, but he was impatient with her.

'It's nothing, just this blasted dyspepsia I seem to keep getting, and then all the fuss of Ralph and Bella coming.' His tone dropped into his usual polite manner. 'But Emma, if I might say so, you look quite beautiful in that pretty dress.'

He put a hand up and touched one of the dark curls at her forehead. Emma felt her first hint of alarm. She stayed silent.

'Emma, I want to know if you are happy with us at School House. Over two months have gone by and I for one, have not regretted asking you to come and look after Alice and George.

'In that time, you've grown from a pretty mining lass into a charming and talented young lady. Your speech has improved and you are doing well with your studies. Miss Paige thinks highly of you and I know that Alice and George have become very fond of you.'

Emma was feeling more and more uncomfortable as she wondered where all this flattery was leading.

He took her hand in his and held it tightly, but even that gesture did not prepare her for his next words. 'You are happy with us here, Emma?'

She nodded dumbly, and then thought fleetingly of Adam knowing that only with him could she be truly happy.

'Good, I am glad to hear it as I want to ask you to stay here permanently, not just as a companion to Alice and George; I want you to be a young mother to them. Emma, I am asking you to be my wife, the next Mrs Peirstone.'

Emma snatched her hand from his. She stood up in panic and hints from the past came flying back to her. Had her parents known this was coming when they had gladly accepted the schoolmaster's money and let her go?

She looked at the man in front of her and saw a fine-looking gentleman of nearly fifty years of age, pale and drawn at that moment, but still with a handsome and intelligent face. He was regarding her fondly and nowhere in his expression could she see any of the harshness which she knew lay somewhere below the surface.

But marriage? Marriage to a man old enough to be her father when she loved someone like Adam? No, never, never. The words screamed out inside of her and she felt the force of them.

She managed to speak politely, hardly knowing where the words came from. 'I'm sorry, Mr Peirstone, I couldn't marry you, it wouldn't be proper.'

Emma had spoken carefully, but Gilbert Peirstone chose not to take any notice of her words.

'Sit down again, Emma. Why ever wouldn't it be proper? It is only natural that I should want to marry again. It is over a year since my Jessie died and I am still a young man.'

'No, I am sorry, Mr Peirstone, I really couldn't.' She realised that she sounded rude and she did sit down, hoping that in her obedience, she could convince him. 'You need to marry someone of your own class, your own age, someone like Mrs Driffield. How could I become a step-mother to Ralph and Adam? It wouldn't be proper, as I said.'

'Emma, I don't want an older woman. I want you, for you are very young and lovely. I am offering you the chance to forget that once you were the daughter of a miner, I am offering you the chance of becoming the wife of the schoolmaster and with the most respected position in Skeneby. You cannot refuse me.'

Emma's reply came quickly. 'The people of Skeneby wouldn't think of it like that, Mr Peirstone. I am a miner's daughter and proud to be so, but everyone would think that I had found my way into your household solely with the idea of becoming the schoolmaster's wife. They would despise me.'

'Emma, they would not despise you, for I would not let them. They do what I say. The whole village does what I expect of them and you are not going to deny me what I want.'

Emma was trembling now, both of his arms were around her, holding her in a clasp which she disliked. She looked him in the face. 'I am not going to marry you, Mr Peirstone.'

The words sounded loud in the clear air of the garden and Emma did not know how she had found the courage to speak out against him.

But he was smiling. 'I have surprised you, Emma. Go away and think it over. In a few weeks time, we will be taking our annual holiday in Whitby. I rent a house there, you know, and Alice and George love the sands and the sea. Come with us and it will give you time to make up your mind. I will return from Whitby feeling certain that you will have agreed to become my wife. Does that suit you, my dear?'

It does suit me, thought Emma, it will give me time. I will be able to tell Adam and if he is no position to marry, then I must consider the proposal. Mr Peirstone has been treating me very kindly and I must assume that the strictness of his nature is felt only in the school.

'Yes, thank you, Mr Peirstone, I would like to come to Whitby very much. I have never seen the sea.'

'I can wait for you, my dear Emma, it will give me great pleasure. You can go now, for I am feeling tired, but I shall look forward to hearing your reply.'

Emma ran quickly back to the house, her mind in a whirl. She flung herself on her bed and found that it was Adam who was in her mind and not his father. How can I marry Mr Peirstone when I love Adam, she asked herself? But if Adam cannot marry me, would I be wise to accept this good opportunity? It is not what I want, but we do not always find the life we really want.

She sat up. I can do nothing until I have seen Adam, she told herself, I will go to Skene Hall tomorrow afternoon. She had made up her mind what to do, but sleep did not come easily.

*   *   *

The following day, she had lunch with Mr Peirstone, but he said very little and she wondered if he was regretting his decision to ask her to be his wife. He looked quite drawn and unwell and she guessed that he was again suffering from what he called his 'blasted dyspepsia'.

As soon as he had gone into his study to have a nap, she said nothing to Mrs Garbutt, but slipped out of the house in the direction of Skene Hall. She had never been inside the hall except for the time when Adam had taken her into the kitchen. She decided to take the higher path across the moor, hoping that perhaps she might see Adam with the sheep or busy in the fields.

But she did not see him anywhere and above the house, all was silent except for the twittering of the skylarks. She reached the back door and called Adam's name, but there was no answering reply and she went inside the kitchen. He was not there and wondering if he might be elsewhere in the house, she started to go from room to room, still calling his name.

It was then she received the shock, for there were many rooms, large and small and with beamed ceilings, but every one was completely empty.

There were old curtains and dirty windows, but no carpets or rugs or even lino; neither was there any furniture except for the odd rickety chair or flimsy table and those covered in dust.

Emma stood at the foot of the broad staircase altogether puzzled. Why is it so empty, she was saying to herself, where does Adam live?

Intrigued, she made her way up the stairs and forgetting now to call Adam's name, but here it was the same story, large empty rooms, no beds or furniture to be seen.

Slowly she went downstairs again realising that she was in an empty house. At the foot of the stairs, she noticed a door slightly ajar.

It was by the front door and she hadn't looked in it before, supposing it to be a cupboard. She pushed the door open and stood in astonishment; again no carpet on the floor, but the room was crammed full of furniture.

A bed in the corner, a large desk and chairs, one easy chair, cabinets full of china and glass and most astonishing of all, along one wall was an enormous glass-fronted bookcase full of old volumes which looked as though they were frequently used.

Intrigued to see that the books were, Emma started towards the bookcase, but as she did so, she heard a sound at the back door. She turned quickly and called Adam's name.

'Adam.'

'Emma?' She could hear that his voice was puzzled. 'Where are you? Whatever are you doing here?'

She flew out of the room towards the back door, into his arms and she burst into tears. The tension had been too much for her.

In the kitchen, Adam held her tightly, pressing his cheek against her dark hair. 'What is it, Emma? Has something gone wrong? Try and tell me.'

'Oh, Adam, I'm so glad you've come, I've been looking for you everywhere.'

'I've been in the fields, I've just popped back to make some tea to take up with me. Come and sit down, we'll both have some tea and you can tell me what has upset you. Something's happened, hasn't it?'

They sat together on the settle and they held earthenware mugs of steaming tea. Emma was glad of the strong drink and the feel of Adam's shoulder next to hers.

'It's Mr Peirstone, Adam, he wants to marry me.'

'Father wants to marry you?' Adam's voice was raised in astonishment and if Emma hadn't been so upset, the expression on his face would have made her laugh. 'Whatever next? What are you saying, Emma? You had better tell me about it.'

She told him the story then and how Mr Peirstone had said he would wait for her reply until they had returned from the holiday in Whitby.

Adam's reaction was instant and positive. 'You can't marry him, Emma, you are going to marry me. I love you, but I have already told you that it will be years before I can afford to be married. I have to put this place in order first.'

He stopped abruptly then spoke very slowly and reluctantly. 'Or do you think it would be a good thing to marry him? You would have a good life and position in Skeneby, better than being married to a poor farmer.

'You haven't seen Skene Hall yet. It's not fit for a dog to live in, let alone someone like you.' He sounded bitter and she looked at him horrified, then she reached up and kissed him on the cheek.

'I have seen the hall, Adam, I walked all around looking for you, upstairs as well. What has happened? Do you mind me asking you? I saw that room by the front door, too, is what where you live?'

She felt the comfort of his arm around her shoulders. 'Yes, it is, Emma. Now do you see why I can't marry you yet?'

'Tell me about it, Adam.'

He sighed. 'It's a long, sad story I'm

afraid. Thirty years ago when Father and Mother were married, my grandparents lived here and everything was very prosperous. My grandmother's family had been mill owners in the West Riding and she was left a fortune. Mother was their only child and they were quite pleased to see her married to the new schoolmaster of Skeneby who was from an old Ellerdale family.

'As children, we had a lovely time visiting Skene Hall, it was a beautiful place in those days . . . ' he broke off, his thoughts in the past.

'What went wrong, Adam?'

'Grandmama and Grandfather died within six months of each other and Mother was left the fortune and Skene Hall, as well. For right or wrong, she decided to strip the hall and move all the furniture to School House, now you know why it is beautifully furnished there.'

'But what about Skene Hall?'

'They couldn't find anyone to take it on and it was left to Will Calvert to run the farm on his own. Then after Mother died and the hall was left to me, Will went off to Farndale and I moved in. As you've discovered, the hall is empty and I live in one room and the kitchen. I'm working all hours to put it on its feet again, but it's an uphill struggle.'

He took her hands in his and gripped them hard. 'Oh, Emma, do you see my problem? I would marry you tomorrow, but I have nothing to offer you . . . it will take years.' He looked at her searchingly. 'No, as much as I love you, I cannot ask it of you.'

He stood up then and walked to the window, staring out in the direction of the moor and the Slake Stones.

Emma hesitated, then went and stood beside him. 'I love you too, Adam, I am used to managing on next to nothing.'

He looked down at her and she thought his expression strange, a mixture of love and anger.

'Emma . . . ' he muttered and took her in his arms.

He had kissed her before, gentle and loving kisses, but this was a fierce and angry kiss and when he finally lifted his head and looked at her, his voice was rough. 'Marry my father, blast you! I want you, Emma, I want you, but I cannot have you!' he muttered and he stormed out of the kitchen.

With tears streaming down her face, Emma watched as he disappeared behind the barns, then she turned and sadly left the house.

7

Slowly, Emma walked back to the School House and when she went in, it was to find a worried-looking Mrs Garbutt.

'Oh, there you are, Miss Emma, thank goodness. I've been looking for you everywhere and you wasn't even in the garden. It's the master, he's been took queer and he's in the drawing-room in quite a way.'

Emma frowned. 'Is it his dyspepsia? He was complaining yesterday and he didn't look at all well.'

Mrs Garbutt seemed flustered. 'He says as it's something he ate at lunch time, but I cannot imagine what for we all had the same and it was only some ham on a plate.'

'I'll go to him,' said Emma quietly and made her way to the drawing-room. She found Mr Peirstone lying stretched out on the large sofa. This was strange in the first place. He looked up as she entered the room.

'Ah, there you are, Emma. I would be glad of your company. Bring that stool over and sit with me.'

As she moved the stool, Emma saw him draw his knees up and grimace with pain.

'It must be more than dyspepsia, Mr Peirstone, have you had these pains before?' she asked him gently.

'On and off for several months,' he told her, 'but they've never been as bad as this. I blame the ham we had for lunch.'

'But we all had it,' was all Emma could find to say. 'Would you like me to send for the doctor?'

He opened his eyes as she spoke and answered her testily. 'No, no, it's just this same old trouble. It came on after lunch, as I said, terrible pains in the stomach, never been so bad. Mrs Garbutt has mixed me some bicarbonate of soda.'

Emma spoke quietly. 'I will heat you some milk, Mr Peirstone, Mother always used to say that warm milk was good for a stomach upset. Perhaps you are right and the ham did disagree with you.' She went into the kitchen returning in a few minutes with a cup of warm milk.

Mr Peirstone seemed glad to sip it and gradually he straightened his legs as though the pain was easing. He suddenly seemed to realise that Emma was standing over him with a look of concern on her face.

★ ★ ★

By dinnertime, he had slept for an hour and announced that he was a lot better and that a good dinner was what he needed. Emma tried to persuade him that it would be better if he tried just to eat a little, but he was inclined to be argumentative and took no notice of what she said.

The following morning, Mr Peirstone

was in a lot of pain again and this time, Emma insisted on sending a boy for the doctor who had to come from Kirbymoorside. Dr Pennock was elderly and had been Gilbert Peirstone's father's medical advisor. Gilbert had known him all his life and had every confidence in him despite his old-fashioned ways.

So it was with surprise, when the trap arrived at the front door of the School House, that Emma saw a young man jump down and carry his bag up to the house.

Aileen let him in and he came into the drawing-room holding out his hand to Mr Peirstone and apologising at the same time. He was not only young, but had good looks with fine fair hair and blue eyes.

'Mr Peirstone, I am sorry that Dr Pennock cannot come. You will probably not know that he has been unwell and has gone over to Baden-Baden to take the waters. My name is Redman, Luke Redman. My practice is in

Ravendale, but I am helping Dr Pennock while he is away.'

Emma liked his calm and open friendliness, but she could see that Mr Peirstone did not.

'There's nothing wrong with me,' he muttered. 'I am sorry to have called you in unnecessarily, I will see Dr Pennock when he returns.'

Emma felt embarrassed and went and stood between the two men. 'I am sorry, Dr Redman, I am Emma Strickland, I look after Mr Peirstone's two younger children. He has been suffering with pains in his stomach since yesterday. We have tried giving him bicarbonate of soda and I get him to drink as much milk as possible, but this morning he has been in considerable pain again.'

'Be quiet, Emma, it is nothing to do with you,' interrupted Gilbert Peirstone. 'I suppose that I had better see this young man now that he is here, but you can go and wait outside.'

She left the room and ten minutes

later, the doctor joined her in the hall. His expression was rueful.

'Miss Strickland, I am afraid that Mr Peirstone does not agree with my diagnosis. It is my opinion that he has a stomach ulcer, it may even be a growth, but he is convinced that it is nothing more than dyspepsia. He will have to watch his diet carefully however much he dislikes it. He should not have any alcohol, but I am afraid that he was not very pleased when I mentioned this. I imagine that he enjoys his glass of claret or brandy!

'I will give you some powders for him, they will contain some morphine to stop the pain and some bismuth. I think perhaps there is no need to tell him about the morphine, the bismuth is a simple antacid and will not alarm him. He should improve quickly, but the further outlook is not good. Do not hesitate to call me again if you should need me.'

Emma looked at him and liked him for his simple outspokenness. 'I am grateful to you, Dr Redman, I have a feeling that he is not going to be an easy patient.

They shook hands and she took him to the front door. 'Goodbye, Miss Strickland, and as I said, I will come whenever you need me.'

'Thank you, Dr Redman.'

She returned to the drawing-room where Mr Peirstone was still lying on the sofa, he was frowning heavily.

'Young jackass,' he said grumpily. 'Says it's a stomach ulcer. Wish I'd waited until old Pennock came back. You can get me a glass of brandy, Emma, that will soon buck me up.'

She was not sure what to say. 'But Dr Redman said that you were not to have any alcohol, Mr Peirstone.'

'Brandy's not going to do me any harm,' he shouted at her. 'Do as I say.'

Reluctantly she poured him a small glass and left him drinking it, he was still scowling and in obvious discomfort.

In the kitchen, she told Mrs Garbutt

what had happened and they decided that Emma should let both Ralph and Adam know of their father's illness. Hastily, she wrote two notes telling them what had happened and then got a boy from the village to run to Skene Hall. She, herself, went to the Post Office to send a letter to Ralph in York.

8

She was surprised when an hour later, Adam arrived at School House. She hardly recognised him. He was dressed in a formal suit and his usually unruly hair had been wetted and brushed neatly back.

He behaved as though he was a stranger, but he was polite and formal and she realised as he spoke that he was very uneasy about meeting his father.

'Emma, thank you for your note. I felt I should come. Do you think Father will see me or will it upset him more? If he is really ill then I feel I should make my peace with him.'

She stood before him feeling rather awkward. 'He is not inclined to believe what the doctor said. It was a young doctor from Ravendale, not Dr Pennock who has apparently attended at School

House for years. I'll go and tell him that you are here.'

Emma turned the handle of the door into the drawing-room. Mr Peirstone was still lying down and he frowned at her. 'Who are you talking to out there?' he asked and there was a tetchy note in his voice.

'It is Adam,' Emma replied. 'Will you see him?'

'Adam has come to see me? He must think I'm on my death bed.'

But Adam had followed Emma into the room and stood by his father's side, shaking him by the hand. 'Father, I'm sorry to see you in poor shape. I thought it was time we let bygones be bygones.'

Mr Peirstone seemed quite pleased at these words. 'Thank you, my boy, thank you. You always did blame me for that business with Bella. I hope you've forgotten her, she would not have made you a good wife. How are things at the Hall?'

Adam drew up a chair and sat at his

father's side. 'It's a struggle, Father, but I shall win.'

Emma, realising that it would be better to leave the two of them on their own, crept out of the room. She couldn't help but wonder what would happen next in this strange week.

Adam left without saying a word to her and the next day, Ralph arrived. He greeted Emma cheerfully.

'Now what's all this about Father? He always did complain about his stomach, but I always put it down to him eating and drinking too much. I hope it is nothing serious.'

'He is in the drawing-room, Mr Ralph,' Emma replied. 'I am afraid you will be shocked at his appearance. He seems to have gone downhill since yesterday and he will keep insisting that brandy will help him when it seems to be doing quite the opposite.'

The next few days were forever after a complete blur to Emma. Mr Peirstone kept to his bed and was in a lot pain. Dr Redman called every day and Mrs

Garbutt said that he looked very serious. Adam came, too, but Emma did not see him and he did not seek her out.

In the evenings, she sat at Mr Peirstone's bedside and held his hand. He had no food for three days and had not even the strength to say her name though Emma thought that he seemed to want to tell her something. When he was at his weakest, he managed to murmur her name and then to say a few words.

'You've been a good girl, Emma. I want to tell you that Alice and George will go to Ralph, so . . . ' but he could say no more.

She bent over and kissed his forehead. 'Sleep well, I am sure that you will feel better in the morning.'

But before nine o'clock next morning, Mr Gilbert Peirstone had died.

Both Ralph and Adam arrived, but Emma saw neither of them. They closeted themselves in Mr Peirstone's study all the morning and Emma stayed with Mrs Garbutt who was beside herself with grief. Both the children were subdued, but they did not cry.

'He were always good to me,' Mrs Garbutt told Emma. 'I know as how he were very strict with the children in school, but he was not a hard man. He thought as how children should be brought up proper.

'He grieved after poor Mrs Peirstone died and now he's gone to join her. And, Miss Emma, Mr Ralph has told me to pack up all Alice and George's belongings in a trunk. He is going to take them back to York to live. Straight away.'

Emma nodded. 'Yes, I do know that. It was the very last thing Mr Peirstone said to me. They both seemed pleased about going live with Ralph and Bella. I have a feeling that they were not very close to their father. They have been quiet, but not upset and seem quite excited about living in York. Do you know when they are going? Will it be after the funeral?'

Mrs Garbutt shook her head. 'No, Mr Ralph came and told me. He doesn't think they should go to their father's funeral, them being so young. So he is taking them to York this afternoon . . . oh, dearie me, I never thought this day would come. I know as how the poor master were poorly, but I never thought it were that bad. Still, he's at peace now and we've got think of ourselves. What will you do, Miss Emma?'

Emma shut her eyes. She did not seem to be able to think. 'I just don't know, Mrs Garbutt. With Alice and George gone, I won't be needed here and my mam and da and the family have gone to join James in Darlington. I suppose I will have to go there . . . I don't want to, though. I don't want to leave Ellerdale if I can help it. I suppose I shall have to try and get a place as a maid somewhere.'

'I'll put in a word for you, Miss Emma, you've been good to Alice and George and the master were fond of you. I know that. Wouldn't have been surprised if he hadn't wanted you to be the next Mrs Peirstone if he had lived, poor gentleman.'

Emma stayed silent. It was Adam who was in her thoughts and not the schoolmaster; and she thought of Adam with a fierce longing. But she knew in her heart that her future did not lie in Skene Hall. Adam had made that very clear.

The grim day wore on. Adam went back to Skene Hall without saying a word to her. The undertakers came and in the afternoon, Emma had to wave off a solemn Alice and George.

After they had gone, the house seemed empty and Emma decided to pack her clothes into her small travelling bag. Tomorrow morning, she told herself, she would either make her way to Darlington or she would go round the big houses to see if anyone needed a maid. I must forget Adam, she kept repeating, and I must forget about being a governess or a teacher. If I can get a place as a maid somewhere, I must count myself fortunate.

She had a quiet word with Mrs Garbutt, Aileen and Nance who were all sad, but Emma felt she must ask if they knew what was going to happen to them.

Mrs Garbutt spoke for them all. 'Mr Ralph says we must close up School House after the funeral, so we've all got to find somewhere to go just the same as you, Miss Emma.

'It's not easy, but Nance says her mother wants her at home as they've got a new baby and Nance doesn't mind, and Aileen, she's going to work in a shop in Kirbymoorside. She's always wanted to work in a shop and her aunt has got a drapers there and is willing to take her on. Aileen wants to be a milliner, she says.'

'But what about you, Mrs Garbutt?'

'I'll be all right, Miss Emma. My sister's husband has died this year and she's lonely and not very well. She's been on at me to go and live with her in

Pickering, so I'm going to give up my cottage for the time being and go and stay with her and see how it works out. It'll be a terrible wrench to leave Skeneby, but Pickering's not that far away. It's been a strange day, it has that and not over yet, but I suppose we'd better do the washing up.'

Emma agreed with her. 'I think I'll have a last walk around the garden, Mrs Garbutt, I've packed my bags ready for tomorrow, unless there's anything you want me to do for you.'

'No, you can go, my love. Aileen and Nance will help me.'

Emma went out of the back door and was glad of the fresh evening air, but she has not even reached the seat when she heard the sound of Mrs Garbutt's voice calling her name.

'Miss Emma, Miss Emma, come quick. There's a gentleman asking for you.'

Emma's heart quickened. Could it be Adam? No, she thought as she hurried back to the house. Adam would have simply come into the garden to look for her.

'In the drawing-room, Miss Emma,' said a Mrs Garbutt who was obviously intrigued by the visitor.

Emma opened the drawing-room door and went in. Standing by the window was Dr Redman.

9

Emma stopped in the doorway of the drawing-room in surprise. Dr Redman turned from the window and smiled. 'Emma, I am glad that you are still here. I thought you might have gone back to your parents' house. It has been a hard and sad week for you.'

He paused and she did not know what to say and was glad when he continued. 'I am sorry I could not have done more for Mr Peirstone, but he was in a bad way by the time I was called in. His death came as no surprise to me.

'Now, I want to ask you what your plans are ... no, don't look so astonished and worried. I am asking you for a very good reason. Are you going back to your home? I understand that the Peirstone children have been taken to York to live with their brother and his wife.'

Emma found her voice at last. 'I am not needed here, Dr Redman, and I must find myself another place. All my family have moved to Darlington, but I feel reluctant to go there. It is hard to imagine living in a big town after being brought up in Ellerdale.'

'You like the countryside?'

'Yes,' she replied, wondering at the question. 'I plan to stay here tonight and then tomorrow, I will go round the big houses to see if I can find a place as a maid.'

'Sit down, Emma, I will sit, too. There is something I would like to suggest to you. It will take a little explaining, so please be patient with me.'

She nodded, mystified.

'I am the only doctor in Ravendale and it was a coincidence that I happened to be helping Dr Pennock out when Mr Peirstone became ill. I am now on my way back to Ravendale and I do not know when I will be this way again as Dr Pennock returns next week.'

He paused. 'But that is all by the way.

Let me tell you something of myself and my family. My wife is called Amy and we have three little children.

'Baby Dolly was born only a few weeks ago and Amy is feeling tired, though she does have someone in to help her with the cleaning and the washing. We soon realised after Dolly was born that Amy would need someone to look after Rose and Andrew. They are our two eldest children though both of them are under five years of age.

'Amy made enquiries in the village, I have searched everywhere, even in Whitby which is our nearest town, but we did not succeed in finding someone suitable. I was beginning to despair. Then chance brought me to Skeneby and to School House and you know the rest of the story, Emma.

'I soon came to realise that you were a very caring person and I am afraid that when Mr Peirstone died this morning and Alice and George were taken to York, my first thought was that

I wondered what you would be planning to do. I knew nothing of your family circumstances, but I decided to come back this evening to see you after I had finished seeing all my patients in Kirbymoorside. Can you guess what I am going to ask you, Emma?'

There was a tense silence in the room as Emma groped for his meaning and wondered if, by some miracle, her thoughts were correct.

'I am asking you, Emma, if you would be prepared to come to Ravendale with me this evening, to meet Amy and to be taken on as a nursery-maid to Rose and Andrew . . . no, let me finish. I realise that you have been acting as a young governess and companion to the Peirstone children, but I have a feeling that you would like it at Priory Cottage with us. It would answer your immediate problem, would it not?'

He smiled then and leaned back in his chair. 'I will give you a few minutes to think it over, but no more than a few minutes for we must be on our way if you are to come with me.'

Emma's thoughts were whirling. How could such good fortune have come to her? She would have to leave Skeneby, but it would still be village life. She would have to forget about Adam for ever, but he had made it clear that he could not marry her for a very long time. There was only one reply she could give to the good doctor.

'Dr Redman, how can I thank you? I feel quite excited for I really did not know what was going to happen to me. I would like to look after your children very, very much, but there are one or two things I must say before I accept.'

'I thought there might be,' he replied with a grin.

But Emma remained serious. 'It is possible that your wife might not like me, that is the first thing, so if I come with you this evening, then I would prefer for it to be on a week's trial. If I am not suitable — and I will certainly do my best — then I will ask you if you would kindly put me on the train at

Whitby so that I can travel to Darlington to join my family.'

She frowned and looked at him directly. 'Does that seem unreasonable to you? Would you accept me on those terms?'

He leaned forward, took her hands in his and gripped them. 'It is very reasonable and I am pleased. I will agree to the week's trial and I know that Amy will, too. But, somehow, I don't think it will be necessary. Now off you go, for you will need to pack up your things and say goodbye to Mrs Garbutt.'

'My bag is packed already,' she told him. 'I was planning to be gone first thing tomorrow morning. But, yes, I must go and see Mrs Garbutt.'

'I will have a walk in the garden,' he said with a smile, 'and I will give you fifteen minutes!'

Emma fetched her bag first and then made her way to the kitchen. Mrs Garbutt was busy clearing up the supper things.

'Oh, Miss Emma, what a day. Will an

end ever come to it? And what had Dr Redman to say . . . ' she stopped and smiled. 'You've got good news, I can see it in your face. That is just what we need, some good news; the poor master passed away, Alice and George gone off with Mr Ralph and poor Mr Adam struggling with that there farm. What is it then, Miss Emma?'

'Oh, Mrs Garbutt, I can hardly believe it. Dr Redman and his wife have been looking for a nursery-maid to their two young children and he has asked me if I would go. I couldn't believe my good fortune and I am going on a week's trial and if I'm not suitable then I will go to Mam and Da in Darlington.

'I can't quite believe it, Mrs Garbutt. It's just as you say. It seems too much all in one day, but I mustn't stay as Dr Redman is taking me to Ravendale now. I've got to say goodbye to you, Mrs Garbutt, and you have been very kind to me while I have been at School House and I never thought it would end like this.'

The two of them were hugging and crying, but Emma remembered something she wanted to say. 'Mrs Garbutt, I don't know if you will see Mr Adam again — apart from at the funeral, I mean — but if he asks after me, will you please tell him that I've gone back to my family in Darlington.'

Mrs Garbutt was puzzled. 'But how is it you've got to know Mr Adam then? He had never come to School House all this time since his mother died and he went to Skene Hall, not until this week, that is. I was right pleased he made up the quarrel before his father died ... oh, poor Mr Peirstone, I can't believe he's gone, that I can't. So how is it you're asking me to give Mr Adam a message and why should he be asking after you?'

Emma decided on a half-truth. 'I used to meet him sometimes on the moor when I took Alice and George for walks, Mrs Garbutt. We liked each other, but that's all there is to it. I want him to think I'm safely back with my family. Will you remember?'

'Yes, Miss Emma, I will. I'll try and see him for you, but it might not be easy for it will be a grand funeral and I will be busy in the kitchen. Then the next day, I shall go off to Ethel's in Pickering like I told you, and the dear old School House will be empty until another schoolmaster comes.'

There were tears in Emma's eyes as she said goodbye to Mrs Garbutt, then she went in search of Aileen and Nance and gave them each a kiss.

In the garden, she joined Dr Redman and together they walked to the front of the house where he helped her into his gig.

The road out of Skeneby passed Skene Hall and Emma looked at the old house sadly. It was not to be, she thought, I must look to a different future now and try and put Adam from my mind — and my heart, she added.

Emma soon forgot Adam and Skene Hall in the pleasure of climbing out of Ellerdale to the high moorland which separated the dale from Ravendale. The two dales were cut off by the moor and there was little communication between them. The moor was at its best in the evening sunshine with the heather just coming into its August glory.

Dr Redman was quiet, but he did tell her a little about the village of Ravendale and of his visits to the widespread farms and cottages which scattered the dale.

As they left the moor behind them and met with green fields and then a steep hill down into the village, Emma began to feel nervous. It all seemed too good to be true, to be offered a new post on the very day she had lost her position at School House.

Dr Redman was cheerful enough, but what kind of reception would she get from his wife, Emma wondered? Mrs Redman knew nothing about her except what her husband might have told her. And would the doctor's wife be expecting Dr Redman to return with a nursery-maid that very day?

The steep, winding lane led into the village and they stopped outside a square stone house of solid proportions and comfort.

'This is Priory Cottage,' Dr Redman said as he helped Emma out of the gig. 'It is said that there was a priory here once, but no trace of it has ever been found, however, the name lives on. Welcome, Emma.'

As they went in the front door, Emma could hear a baby crying, then two small children ran out to meet them calling 'Dada, Dada.' They were followed by a tall young woman not a lot older than Emma.

Dr Redman had his hand on Emma's arm. 'Emma, this is my dear wife, Amy.' He looked at his wife. 'Amy, Mr Peirstone died this morning and Emma was about to search for a place as a maid somewhere in Ellerdale.'

Emma interrupted in an urgent whisper. 'Dr Redman, I don't think I'd better come here. It was very kind of you to think of it, but Mrs Redman should have had a chance to see me first. To see if I would be suitable, I mean.'

Amy Redman heard the soft words and she smiled. She looked at Emma and made up her mind in a glance that her husband had been right to bring the girl to her. She took a step forward and held out her hand.

'Emma,' she said quietly and with authority. 'I am going to call you Emma and I want to say that you are very welcome at Priory Cottage. We have been trying so hard to find someone suitable and when Luke told me of your position at School House, I was very much encouraged.

'I am sorry that you have had such a worrying time during Mr Peirstone's illness. Luke knew from the start that there was little hope for the school-master. I am very pleased that he has brought you back with him this evening.'

Emma held on to the hand which had been offered. 'Mrs Redman, it is most generous of you when you know nothing about me. But I am used to small children as I have many small brothers and sisters, so I will do my best.

'I must tell you that I have insisted that I come to you on trial for a week, then if you are not pleased with me, Dr Redman has promised to put me on the train to take me to my family who have moved from Skeneby to Darlington.'

Luke Redman had disappeared and came back holding a baby. 'I think Baby Dolly had some wind,' he said cheerfully. 'She is all right now.'

Emma was talking to the two young children whose names were Rose and Andrew, Rose being a pretty little three-year-old and Andrew, at nearly five, was very much like his father in looks.

Luke looked at the two of them with great affection in his eyes. 'Now, you two, it is your bedtime. I am sure your mama has kept you up until I returned and now I have brought Emma with me. She will look after you and I hope you will like her.' He turned to Emma. 'Amy put them to bed tonight and you will have all day tomorrow to get to know them.'

★ ★ ★

Emma soon discovered that looking after the two children was to be her sole duty. Dr Redman had found a woman from the village to help his wife with the cooking and cleaning. Mrs Hoggarth turned out to be a very friendly soul and reminded Emma of Mrs Garbutt.

Amy settled the children, then took Emma up to a small room at the top of the house reached by a narrow wooden stair. 'I hope this will suit you,' she said. 'It is only the attic, but this is not a big house and all the other bedrooms are in use.'

Emma looked around her. It was a small room, but it had pretty curtains and a coverlet on the bed to match.

There was a thick rug on the lino, a tall chest of drawers and in the corner, a small wash-stand with a marble top. The furniture gave the little room a rather crowded look, but to Emma, it seemed to spell comfort.

She walked to the window and gave a sigh as she looked up the dale in the late evening sunshine. She turned to the doctor's wife and held out a hand towards her in gratitude.

'Mrs Redman, I will never be able to thank you enough. When Mr Peirstone died this morning, I did not know what was to become of me. I even packed my bag ready to leave School House and then Dr Redman came. I think that both of you were sent from heaven and I will do my very best for you.'

Amy Redman was looking pleased. 'I have the feeling that your misfortune is to be to our advantage,' she said. 'And, Emma, please will you call me Amy. I would like that and I know that my husband would ask you to call him Luke.'

Emma gave a shy smile. 'Thank you, Amy.'

The three of them had supper together and Emma went up to her room. She slept very well and next morning felt rather strange as she went downstairs in search of Amy who she found getting the breakfast.

In the kitchen, Emma went up to the large table in the centre of the spacious room. 'Mrs Redman, please let me help you,' she said.

Amy smiled. 'What did you call me?' she asked teasingly.

Emma grinned. 'It seems forward of me, Amy, but I will do it if you wish.' She paused. 'Shall I cut the bread and butter?'

'Yes, you may if you like. You will think that I am a very idle housewife. I have Mrs Hoggarth who comes in to do the cooking and the washing, then once a week, her daughter Janet who is big strong girl and still lives at home, does all the cleaning for me. So I am very lucky.'

Emma looked at her. The doctor's wife looked quite young, but she seemed mature and sensible. 'You have Dr Redman to think of as well as the children and I expect you visit in the village when you can.' She was not sure if she had said the right thing, but Amy gave her an appreciative glance.

'Yes, being the doctor's wife does bring some duties with it and I like to help Luke when I can. He is so busy and so good and is always wanting me to take baskets of food to one or other of the poorer families in the village. He sees so much and never gets paid, but then he has his rich patients, too, so it must balance out.'

She paused. 'Emma, I think that the two of us will get on well together. Tell me about the children at School House in Skeneby and I believe you helped in the school, too. You must be a very studious person. I never was, my governess despaired of me!'

Emma laughed at Amy's rueful remark and they almost forgot about getting the breakfast they were so busy talking. Then Rose and Andrew appeared to say that they were hungry and they thought Baby Dolly was waking up.

Life gradually changed for Emma. The days seemed idyllic at Priory Cottage and as she got to know Ravendale, she began to love it as much as she did Ellerdale. Although the two dales were not far apart, there was only the rough moorland road which linked the two and they might have been different worlds.

Communication between the dales was rare and Emma sometimes marvelled how it was that Dr Redman — she had learned to call him Luke — had come to visit Skeneby at all.

She soon learned that country doctors were used to travelling long distances, sometimes in a gig, but more often on horseback when moorland villages and isolated farms needed a doctor.

She also got used to the fact that

Luke was rarely at home and when he did arrive at Priory Cottage in the late evening, tired and hungry, she was careful to be in her bedroom so that he and Amy could have some time together.

Amy insisted that she had one afternoon off and when it was fine, Emma loved to explore the area. She soon learned that by taking a track up from the middle of the village, she was soon on Ravendale Rigg.

It was a long ridge stretching the whole length of the dale and from it there were glorious views; on clear days, Emma discovered that she could catch a glimpse of the sea at Whitby.

It was when she was up on the Rigg that Emma felt her moments of sadness. At the Redman house, she was always kept too busy to dwell on the past, but walking freely and solitary, her thoughts would fly to Adam; they were thoughts of an aching melancholy. Still fresh in her memory, was his angry kiss and his blunt statement that he could not marry her.

Sometimes, she longed to see him, but she knew that it was impossible. She had been so near to love and yet so far and she found it more than difficult to face up to the idea that she had lost Adam for ever. She still wore the pendant he had given her and she would touch it lovingly even though she knew now that she had no right to it.

Time passed very quickly for Emma and they were soon into autumn, during August, Dr Redman had given himself a week off and they all went to Whitby. Amy said that it was no holiday for Emma, but Emma thought otherwise.

She had longed to see the sea and enjoyed every minute of the week on the sands with Rose and Andrew. Dolly had grown into a strong baby and they succeeded in hiring a wicker basket so that she could be carried on to the beach with them.

After that, no news came from Ellerdale and Emma often wondered if the school was open again with its new schoolmaster. She wondered, too, how Adam was faring in putting Skeneby Hall to rights.

Early in October, Luke was once again called over to Kirbymoorside to help Dr Pennock. On his way home through Skeneby, he was prompted to stop at School House. He knew that Emma would be interested to know if the new schoolmaster was installed.

He knocked at the front door and it was opened, to his great surprise, by Mrs Garbutt. He had thought Emma to say that she had gone to live with her sister in Pickering.

'Why, if it isn't Dr Redman,' exclaimed Mrs Garbutt. 'Well, I never did. Have you got any news of Miss Emma. I often think of her.'

'She is well, thank you, Mrs Garbutt. I called to see if the new schoolmaster had arrived. I didn't expect to find you here.'

'Well, you must come in and have a cup of tea with me. Mr Franklin is over at the school and Mrs Franklin is down the village somewhere. I think as how she said she were going to do the flowers for the church. Now, do you mind sitting in the kitchen with me and I'll tell you all about it. And you can tell me if Miss Emma went to Darlington or not.'

10

Sitting in the kitchen and drinking tea with Mrs Garbutt, Luke thought he would never get a word in. But he listened to her story with patience and, he had to admit it, with interest and curiosity.

'As soon as Mr and Mrs Franklin moved in, they was looking for a housekeeper. They've got two boys, twelve and fourteen years old they are, and at school in York. They board there all week and come to Kirbymoorside with the journeyman for the weekends. Mr Franklin fetches them home from there.

'Well, it turns out that Mrs Franklin is a certificated teacher and she goes over to school to help Miss Paige just like Miss Emma used to do. So, as I said, they was looking for a cook-housekeeper and there was no-one in the village who would suit. So the dear vicar suggested that I might like to come back and Mr Franklin came to see me. I didn't hesitate, Dr Redman.

'My sister was a lot better and getting over the loss of her husband and I found it very quiet. So back I came and here I am and it's right good to see you. Now you must tell me about Miss Emma. I've thought of her often, wondering what had happened to her.

'Emma has stayed with us at Ravendale, Mrs Garbutt,' Luke told her. 'She is very good with the children and I am pleased to say that she and my wife are firm friends. There was never any question of her going to Darlington after she had been with us for a few days and doing so well.

'She has spoken to Amy of Mr Adam Peirstone, I believe that she must have been very fond of him, but that they had some sort of quarrel. I would like to take her news of him.

Mrs Garbutt was nodding. 'I didn't know of it because Mr Adam didn't come to School House, but it seems she used to see him up on the moor. Whether it was a romance or not I couldn't say, but when she left here with you that night, she told me to tell Mr Adam — if he asked after her, that was — that she had gone home to her family. So when I next saw him, that's what I said — it could have been the truth for all I knew.'

'And Adam? Is he still farming at Skene Hall? I understand it was rather a struggle.'

Mrs Garbutt gave a broad smile. 'Now there's a happy outcome, Dr Redman, I'll tell you about it if you don't mind a long story. I was sorry to lose the master like that, but it were a good day for Mr Adam.'

'I would be pleased to hear about it, Mrs Garbutt. Take your time.'

'Well, it were like this. When the will was read, it turned out that Mr Peirstone — bless the dear man — had left the bulk of his money to Mr Adam and all the furniture from School

House as well. It was in the will that Mr Ralph had already benefited from his mother's fortune and now it was Adam's turn. They'd quarrelled, you know, Mr Peirstone and Adam. It was after Mrs Peirstone died and the master didn't want Mr Adam to turn farmer. But Skene Hall was his so that was that.'

She paused, but Luke said nothing.

'It all took a while to be settled and then Mr and Mrs Franklin were ready to move into School House and the furniture had to be moved to Skene Hall. That's where it all came from in the first place and all of it the finest quality brought over from the hall when Mrs Peirstone's parents died. I don't know if you knew that was her home, she were born of at Skene Hall were Mrs Peirstone — but of course you never knew her.

'Quite the lady she were and a nicer lady you couldn't wish to find in the whole of Yorkshire. Now what was I saying . . . oh yes, about the furniture being moved to Skene Hall. Such a day it were and all. Mr Adam brought a farm wagon and it was all piled up, I think every man in the village turned out to help him.' Again the pause as she took breath, but still Luke stayed silent.

'Now you must realise that Skene Hall was neglected after Mrs Peirstone's parents died. Old Will Calvert lived there as he was running the farm until Mr Adam took it over. But the farm were real run down and Mr Adam working so hard to put it to rights. I do believe it were said he lived in just one room and the rest of that old house left to the dust and the mice.

'So it was that Skene Hall were in no fit state for any furniture, but you see, the men who was helping they brought their wives and it was all cleared out and cleaned, windows, curtains, everything. Then the carpets went down and the furniture was took in and it looked lovely. The old place looked just as it did in Mr Adam's grandparents' day, I really thought he would cry when he saw it all.

'I cooked a big tea for the helpers, then I came back to School House to help Mr and Mrs Franklin settle in here. Well, it's been a long story, Dr Redman, and I'd be that pleased if you would tell it all to Miss Emma. And give her my love and tell her I think she's a lucky young lady.'

Luke thanked Mrs Garbutt and said goodbye and drove away from School House very thoughtfully. I think, he was saying to himself as he went through the village, that before I say anything to Emma, I will try and find out Mr Adam Peirstone's side of the story. It may be that a little matchmaking is needed, though, of course, it might mean that we would lose Emma. We shall see.

He stopped at Skene Hall and a young maid let him in. She said that she would try and find Mr Peirstone, she thought he was in the stackyard.

Luke sat in the drawing-room, looking round him with pleasure at the priceless pieces of furniture he remembered seeing at School House.

Then Adam came into the room. 'Dr Redman,' he exclaimed and seemed pleased. 'How very good of you to call. I'm sorry, I'm not really fit to be seen in the drawing-room, but you will know that I farm Skene Hall and I had no time to change.'

Adam, in fact, was looking very well. Still tanned from the summer sun and the time spent out of doors, he was handsome in corduroys and a brown flannel shirt open at the neck. His feet were in socks as though he had taken off muddy boots to come and greet his visitor.

'I will ask Lucy to bring us some wine, Dr Redman, or would you prefer a glass of ale?'

'Some wine would be most acceptable,' replied Luke. 'I am sorry I have called unexpectedly, but I have been over in Kirbymoorside helping Dr Pennock out again. I stopped at School House as I was coming through

Skeneby and I was pleased to find Mrs Garbutt still there. She told me of your good fortune, it must please you to see the furniture back in its rightful place.'

Adam nodded. 'Yes, this is just as it used to be, I am pleased to say and I no longer have to live in one room as I was doing. The farm is slowly picking up and I have been able to take on two men and a lad from the village, so that is a great help to me.'

Luke said the next words very deliberately. 'You plan to bring a wife to Skene Hall, Mr Peirstone?'

Adam shook his head. 'No, I don't. I had hoped to marry once, but it went wrong. I will tell you. It was young Emma Strickland who looked after my younger brother and sister at School House. I wanted to marry her, but I could offer marriage to no-one. I had no money and Skene Hall was empty of furniture, carpets, everything. I did get it all back under the terms of Father's will as you can see, it's all looking as it should do.

'I've lost Emma and I don't want anyone else. Mrs Garbutt told me that Emma had gone back to her parents in Darlington so at least I know where she is and that she is cared for. She has probably met someone else by now and has forgotten all about Adam Peirstone and Skene Hall.'

The last words were said rather bitterly and Luke knew it was time to speak the truth.

'Adam — I will call you Adam if you don't mind, you will discover why in a moment — please be prepared for a shock, but what I hope will be happy news.'

Adam stared. 'What do you mean?'

'Emma Strickland did not go to her parents in Darlington. She was all prepared to go and I would have taken her if she had wished it. But I must tell you that my wife, Amy, and I were in need of a nursery-maid for our two young children. So on the day Mr Peirstone died — you had come back to Skene Hall by that time — I called at

School House and asked Emma if she would come to Ravendale as our nursery-maid.

'She was very thankful to be asked, but would only come on one condition — it was that if she did not prove suitable, I was to put her on the train for Darlington and she would go back and live with her parents . . . '

Adam could not stop his interruption. 'Do you mean . . . are you going to say that she is not in Darlington?'

Luke smiled. 'That is so. She proved to be very good with Rose and Andrew, she stayed with us in Ravendale and she and my wife have become good friends.'

'I can't believe it. To think she has been in Ravendale all this time. Oh, I am so pleased, so pleased for her.' He stared at Luke. 'You have called to tell me all this. Does it mean that Emma has spoken of me to your wife?'

'Yes, I think it all came out gradually and I believe the truth of it to be that you had a quarrel.'

'It wasn't a quarrel,' replied Adam.

'The truth is that my father had asked Emma to be his wife and the thought of it dismayed her. She turned to me, but although I loved her, I was in no position to offer marriage to anyone. She told me that she loved me, but I said it was impossible and that she would be better off married to my father . . . ' he stopped as though his thoughts were back in the past.

'I rushed off then and left her in tears, I shall never forget it. Then you know the rest, for Father became ill and I didn't see Emma on her own again . . . I can't believe it, I just can't believe it. What shall I do, Dr Redman?'

'You would still like to marry her?'

'Yes, I would,' said Adam with no hesitation.

Luke was thoughtful. 'I think the best thing would be for you to come and see her in Ravendale. Would you like to join us for luncheon next Sunday?'

'Thank you very much,' said Adam eagerly. 'Yes, I would like to do that, if you are sure your wife will agree to it.'

'Yes, I know she will. She will not like to lose Emma, but Amy would be pleased to see her settled with you here at Skene Hall. Emma's happiness comes first with both of us. We have become very fond of her ... ' he stopped and looked at Adam. 'You are thinking of something.'

'That's right. I cannot be sure of her feelings after our last meeting and I don't want her refusing to see me just because I said I couldn't marry her the last time we met. What do you think?'

Luke smiled. 'We will let it be a surprise and I think I can be sure of the outcome.' He rose from his chair and shook hands with Adam. 'We will look forward to seeing you at Priory Cottage on Sunday morning. You cannot mistake it, for it is a solid stone house right in the centre of Ravendale and not far from the bridge over the river.'

Adam saw him out, then went back to his work with joy in his heart.

Luke drove back to Ravendale feeling quite pleased with himself, and Amy was pleased, too, though sad at the thought that she might have to lose Emma.

★　★　★

The day that Adam rode over to Ravendale was one of October's wild and windy days with sudden outbreaks of heavy rain, but he wore his heavy waterproof cape and managed, for the most part, to keep dry.

Inside Priory Cottage, Emma was sitting at the kitchen table giving the children their mid-morning drinks when there came a sound of a horse in the lane outside and then a knock at the front door. She heard Amy let someone in and raised her head in alarm when she recognised a voice she knew so well.

'Mrs Redman? I am pleased to meet you. I am Adam Peirstone of Skene Hall and your husband kindly invited me to come over to Ravendale today. He told me that you have Emma Strickland here and I would very much like to see her. I apologise for my wet condition, I didn't choose the best of days for riding over to Ravendale.'

Emma felt that she could not move, but she listened to Amy's pleasant reply.

'You are Emma's Adam, I am so glad that you have come. Do please come in.'

Adam stood in the kitchen doorway. 'Emma,' he said and his voice, though cautious, seemed to carry a note of gladness and expectancy.

Emma panicked. She could not face Adam. How did he know that she was here? And why had he come? When she spoke, her voice was shrill and the words tumbled out as though she did not know what she was saying.

'Adam, what are you doing here? I don't want to see you, I have nothing to say . . . you can't want to see me either. I won't stay . . . '

She turned away from him and rushed out of the back door, running as fast as she could through the rain, across the fields and up towards the Rigg. Adam's face was before her, but her only thought was to escape from all the heartaches and explanations.

Back in the house, Amy looked at Adam in dismay and then acted quickly. 'I'm sorry, Mr Peirstone — Adam — I don't know why Emma has run off. We thought your visit would be a nice surprise for her. Go after her, take your horse up the track at the side of the house and you will find yourself on top of Ravendale Rigg. Emma always goes up there, she will be running across the fields.

'Go quickly to the top of the track where the heather moor starts, you will see an old stone barn. Make for that, I am certain that Emma will do the same . . . ' she was pushing him out of the front door and he looked bewildered. 'No, wait a moment, take Emma's cloak, she is in only her thin dress and she will be soaked through.'

She put a heavy woollen cloak into his hands and shut the door behind him, giving a sigh of relief when she heard the sound of the horse's hoofs on the stones of the lane.

'Let it be all right,' she gave a silent prayer. 'Please let it be all right.'

In the meantime, Emma was struggling for breath as she reached the last steep slope up to the Rigg. She was half-walking, half-running through the heather, now brown and rough after its summer colour. Why has he come? How did he know where I was? What does he want?

The question went round and round in her brain until she felt dizzy; by now, her dress was soaked through and clinging to her. The rain beat down even more heavily as she reached the top and the wind on that open moor was howling; thankfully she caught sight of the old barn. I'd better shelter for a while, she told herself, and get my breath back. Then try and think what to do next.

What she had not been prepared for as she reached the shelter of the barn was that as soon as she stopped moving, she would start to feel cold. She stood at the barn entrance — the door had long since disappeared — and gazed at the tempestuous scene outside. The view she usually enjoyed from this favourite spot was completely blotted out by the rain.

She started to shiver and did not know how to get warm. I'll have to run down the track to the lane, she was thinking, I've got to get out of these wet things and Adam will probably be gone by now.

Then she realised what she had done. He must have come to see me specially and he sounded so glad. I ran away, I am a coward. I should have talked to him, listened to what he had to say. Now he'll go back to Skene Hall and I've lost my chance for ever. What a fool I am.

When she heard the sound of a horse coming up the track, she thought she must be deluded; no-one would come up here in this weather, she told herself.

'Emma, are you there? Emma, Emma.'

She heard her name and knew that it was Adam's voice, but she thought her shivering fit must have brought on a fever.

Then he was in front of her, leading his horse in to the barn, standing tall and strong in his wet cloak, looking at her.

'Adam.'

'Emma, why ever did you run away?'

'Oh Adam.' It was all she could find to say as she looked at him.

He opened his arms to her and she ran into them as though it was the only thing she wanted or needed to do.

She hid her head against his chest, very near to tears. He held her close and felt her give a shiver.

'Emma, my love, you are wet through and shivering. Look, Mrs Redman has given me your woollen cloak, I've kept it under my waterproof and it is quite dry. Wrap it round you quickly.'

He dropped his own wet cape to the ground and tenderly wrapped her in her dry cloak, then he folded his arms around her and she began to feel warm again.

'Why did you run away from me, Emma?' he asked her again.

'I was frightened, I couldn't understand how you knew where I was and why you had come.'

He laid his cheek against her wet head. 'We are not going to stand here getting colder and colder. We have a lot of talking to do and it's going to be done in comfort. I'll take you up on the horse and we'll be back at the Redmans' in minutes.'

Emma was still shivering and knew he was right; she looked into his grey eyes which were kind with concern for her, and she knew with a certainty that she would do whatever he asked her to do, always.

She felt gentle lips on hers and knew once again the delight of his kiss.

'Emma,' he whispered. 'I love you, I have never stopped loving you all this time. Can you possibly still love me?'

She managed a smile and pressed close to his heart. 'I do love you, Adam, I do, but I must talk to you.'

He silenced her with another kiss holding her close, his hands round her waist. She gave a shiver and whether it was of delight or cold she did not know, but Adam was hugging her to him.

'I'm a brute,' he said brusquely. 'We must get you home.' And he wrapped the cloak around her, picked her up and put her on the back of his horse.

Emma shivered and laughed at the same time when he joined her and wrapped her completely in his waterproof. She clung to him all the way back to Priory Cottage and when they arrived, there was much fuss and laughter.

Adam was told to sit by the fire in the living-room while Amy got out the tub in the kitchen and made Emma immerse herself in the hot water until all her signs of shivering had disappeared. She told her to go upstairs and put on one of her prettiest dresses and when Emma came downstairs again, she shyly joined Adam in front of the fire.

It was a very happy Sunday lunch and just for once, Rose and Andrew were allowed to sit up at the big table in the dining-room. They had to have cushions on their chairs to make them higher, but they were very well-behaved and Emma was proud of them.

After lunch, Amy insisted that Adam and Emma should have the living-room to themselves. Luke said he would have a nap in his study and Amy went up to the nursery with the children.

As the door shut behind them, Emma met Adam's eyes with a laugh. 'Did you ever meet such kind people? They are saints, both of them.'

Adam smiled. 'We have so much to talk about, Emma. I cannot believe that I have found you again after all this time. I imagined you safely in Darlington with your mother and father — and possibly a new sweetheart! I couldn't believe it when Luke told me you were here.'

Emma looked at him. 'But why didn't you let Luke tell me you were coming today?'

Adam's expression was rueful. 'I wasn't sure enough. We had parted unhappily and then Father died and I didn't see you again. I thought I would let it be a surprise — and then you ran away!'

'I'm sorry, Adam. I suppose I've loved you all this time and I couldn't bear to see you if you were going to tell me again that you couldn't marry me. It was asking too much.' She looked at him carefully, then smiled. 'Adam Peirstone, you are looking prosperous. Did your father leave you some money?'

Adam nodded. 'He did and I have a nice surprise for you. But it must wait. Emma, I loved you from the first moment I met you at the Slake Stones. Then I thought I had lost you and I vowed that I would never marry anyone else. Now we are here together again so

I can say it properly. I love you, Emma, but I am not going to ask you to marry me until you have seen Skene Hall.'

They were sitting together on the sofa and Emma reached up and put her arms around his neck. 'I love you just as much as ever, Adam, and I will be patient, I promise. It is just good to have found you again.'

Adam gave her a quick kiss. 'Listen, Emma. We will tell the Redmans and then I will ride back to Skeneby. Tomorrow, I will bring the gig and I will take you over to Skene Hall. Then you can tell me if you want to marry me or not.'

'Oh, Adam, I would marry you if we had to live in one room, I wouldn't mind a bit. As long as you have enough money to keep the farm going, for I know that is what you want to do.

'And you won't mind being a farmer's wife and not a schoolteacher?' he teased her.

She kissed him again. 'I wouldn't mind being this farmer's wife,' she said laughing, and she got up. 'Come along, let us go and find Luke and Amy.'

The Redmans were both pleased to see the pair so happy, but Amy looked at Emma sadly. 'I shall lose you, Emma, what shall I do?'

Emma was thoughtful. 'I am thinking of Nance, she was one of the maids at School House. She didn't look for another position, but went back to her home because her mother had a new baby and needed her help. She is such a good girl, Amy, I am sure you would like her. I do think you should give her a try — if I marry Adam, that is.'

They all laughed at this and Amy asked what she meant.

Emma gave a chuckle, but looked serious. 'Adam refuses to ask me to marry him until I have seen Skene Hall, it was derelict last time I was there. If you could spare me tomorrow, Amy, Adam will come over to fetch me. He is being very mysterious about it, so I will have to go!'

'Yes, of course, Emma, I am only too

168

pleased about it, except for losing you, that is. But if you will tell us where Nance lives, then Luke can go and ask her.'

Adam left then and Emma waited impatiently for the following day.

When Adam arrived with the gig, he was in a teasing mood and Emma did not know quite what to expect when they arrived at Skene Hall. They went in by the front door and immediately, Emma felt the shock of the transformation.

Every piece of furniture, even the pictures were familiar to her and she turned to Adam with shining eyes. 'You have moved all the furniture from School House, Adam. It looks beautiful in this old house, no wonder you kept it as a surprise.'

He showed her over the whole house and Emma could hardly believe it; from being a shabby old farmhouse, it had been changed into an elegant hall.

As they came down the stairs again, Adam pulled her into his arms. 'I can see that you are pleased with everything, Emma, and it needs only you to make the house complete. Now I can ask you properly, I am a wealthy farmer and I own Skene Hall. All I need now is a beautiful wife and I think I have her in my arms. I told you I loved you yesterday. Emma, will you marry me? Now I can ask you at last.'

Emma was smiling happily. 'I would have married you when you had nothing, Adam, for I love you very much. But it is wonderful to see Skene Hall looking so splendid and you so prosperous.' She gave him a kiss. 'Yes, I do love you, Adam, and yes, I would like to marry you.'

Adam and Emma were married a month later, exactly the time it took to call the banns. It seemed the whole village was in the church for the wedding and most of them returned to Skene Hall for a splendid wedding breakfast prepared by Mrs Garbutt, whom Emma had been delighted to find still at School House.

Adam could not spare a lot of time away from the farm, but it was a very happy Emma who went off to Scarborough for a few days by the sea with her new husband.

THE END

RETURN TO HEATHERCOTE MILL

Jean M. Long

Annis had vowed never to set foot in Heathercote Mill again. It held too many memories of her ex-fiancé, Andrew Freeman, who had died so tragically. But now her friend Sally was in trouble, and desperate for Annis' help with her wedding business. Reluctantly, Annis returned to Heathercote Mill and discovered many changes had occurred during her absence. She found herself confronted with an entirely new set of problems — not the least of them being Andrew's cousin, Ross Hadley . . .

THE COMFORT OF STRANGERS

Roberta Grieve

When Carrie Martin's family falls on hard times, she struggles to support her frail sister and inadequate father. While scavenging along the shoreline of the Thames for firewood, she stumbles over the unconscious body of a young man. As she nurses him back to health she falls in love with the stranger. But there is a mystery surrounding the identity of 'Mr Jones' and, as Carrie tries to find out who he really is, she finds herself in danger.

LOVE IN LUGANO

Anne Cullen

Suzannah Lloyd, sculptor and horticulturist, arrives at an exhibition in Lugano which is showing some of her orchid sculptures. There she meets Mr Di Stefano, who offers her a job managing the grounds of his estate and orchid collection. Working closely with Mr Di Stefano's right hand man, Dante Candurro, she falls in love with him — but overhears his plans to steal the Di Stefano art collection. Feeling betrayed by further deception, can she ever learn to trust him?

THE CROSS AND THE FLAME

Roberta Grieve

While the Great Plague rages through London, Hester dreams of her sailor sweetheart Jonathan, despite being promised in marriage to her father's friend — the odious Thomas Latham. The deaths of her mother and baby brother bring guilty relief when the wedding is postponed. Then Jonathan returns to the news that Hester has died in the plague. Will he discover the deception before she is forced to marry a man who has no place in her heart?

MOTHER OF THE BRIDE

Zelma Falkiner

Kay Sheridan enjoys owning The Tea Cosy gift shop and tea-rooms. But for her, life has become quite hectic. A developer is threatening to disturb her tranquil village, and her landlord is demanding an increase in the rent of her premises that could close her down. Then her impetuous daughter surprises her with wedding plans, which will mean the return of her estranged husband. Will Kay be able to hide her unchanged love for him?

A LESSON IN LOVE

Shirley Heaton

Attractive widow Carol meets Paul on a campsite in France. After her return from holiday she discovers that he is the new tutor at her art class. Their friendship develops but, suspecting Paul may already have a partner, she is reluctant to make a commitment. During a visit to her health club, company director Simon introduces himself and later wines and dines her. Torn between the two, it takes a dangerous encounter for her to acknowledge her true love.